Demetri's Picture Perfect Christmas

Ike Ojukwu

Published by Ike Ojukwu, 2024.

This is a work of fiction. Similarities to real people, places, or events are entirely coincidental.

DEMETRI'S PICTURE PERFECT CHRISTMAS

First edition. November 1, 2024.

Copyright © 2024 Ike Ojukwu.

ISBN: 979-8227278678

Written by Ike Ojukwu.

To my family and friends, Thank you for your unwavering love, support, and laughter. This story wouldn't exist without your inspiration, encouragement, and belief in me. You are my heart, my joy, and my motivation every day.

Chapter 1: A Job Offer and a Race Against Time

Shreveport, Louisiana was a city that dressed in twinkling lights during the holidays, transforming the streets into a postcard-perfect winter wonderland—minus the snow. It hadn't snowed in years, but that didn't stop the locals from decorating like they were expecting a blizzard any second. Every lamppost was wrapped in red ribbons and pine garlands, storefronts had frosted their windows with fake snow, and the air was thick with the scent of hot cocoa, cinnamon, and desperation as last-minute shoppers darted in and out of stores.

Inside his cluttered office, **Demetri Jameson** was anything but in the holiday spirit. He leaned forward at his desk, eyes glued to the computer screen, fingers moving over the keyboard like a man possessed. Photos of families, laughing and smiling in front of holiday trees, stared back at him as he worked his editing magic, turning each picture into the kind of memory that his clients would hang proudly on their walls.

But Demetri wasn't smiling.

The stack of unopened mail beside him had grown into a small mountain over the last few weeks. It was easy to ignore when you were constantly drowning in work. His office was a mess—empty coffee cups balanced precariously on top of each other, invoices stuffed in between camera lenses, and a discarded Santa hat sat atop a pile of memory cards. It was a chaotic reflection of Demetri's life—a successful photographer, perhaps, but one who was in the middle of a full-blown personal and financial crisis.

Click, Clank, Click, Clank, red high heels, just like Dorothy's step one after the other. Swishing wide hips in a red Mrs. Claus skirt cascaded down a serene hall towards an office door labeled " Kreative Photography" "318".

"Demetri, you really need to look at these." **Sharon**, his assistant, stepped into the office, her arms laden with yet another stack of mail. Her face was a mixture of exasperation and worry, like a mom who'd told her child ten times to clean his room but knew it would never happen.

Demetri waved her off without looking up. "Just leave them on the desk, Sharon. I'll get to it later."

"You've been saying that for weeks." Sharon dropped the letters onto an already precarious pile. "Some of these are from months ago. And one of them is from the IRS."

That got his attention. His hands froze on the keyboard, and his eyes flicked toward the stack of mail.

"The IRS?"

Sharon nodded, folding her arms across her chest. "It's marked urgent. I thought you might want to look at it before, I don't know, your entire life goes up in flames?"

Demetri sighed, finally tearing his eyes away from the computer screen. "Fine, fine. Give me the damn letter."

Sharon fished out the thick envelope, handing it to him like it was a grenade ready to explode. "You're welcome," she said, her tone making it clear that she wasn't going to let him brush this off.

With a sense of dread creeping up his spine, Demetri ripped open the envelope and pulled out the contents. His eyes scanned the letter, and with each line, his stomach dropped lower and lower. He had known things were bad, but this... this was a nightmare.

"I owe over a hundred grand?" His voice barely registered above a whisper.

Sharon nodded sympathetically. "Yeah, that's what happens when you ignore the IRS for months."

"I didn't even know about this!" Demetri snapped, tossing the letter onto his desk. "Why the hell didn't you give me this sooner?"

"I did!" Sharon shot back, her voice rising in frustration. "Three months ago! You were too busy to care then. You're always too busy."

Demetri opened his mouth to argue but stopped himself. She was right. He'd been so wrapped up in his work that everything else—his finances, his family, his life—had fallen apart around him. He rubbed a hand over his face, exhaustion pulling at his features. He hadn't even started Christmas shopping yet, and King, his nine-year-old son, had been dropping hints about a new Bronny James basketball jersey for weeks.

Christmas. How had it crept up on him so fast?

As if on cue, his phone rang, buzzing insistently from where it sat on his cluttered desk. He snatched it up without checking the caller ID. "Demetri speaking."

"Demetri! I'm glad I caught you." The voice on the other end was familiar, but he couldn't quite place it.

"Who's this?" Demetri asked, rubbing his temples.

"It's **Marcy** from **Bureau Luxe**. I've got a huge opportunity for you."

Demetri sat up straighter, the name triggering instant recognition. Bureau Luxe was one of the biggest fashion brands in the country, and they'd been on his radar for years. If this was what he thought it was...

"Go on," he said, trying to keep the excitement out of his voice.

"We had a last-minute cancellation. Our photographer for the holiday campaign dropped out. We need someone to step in immediately. It's a full-day shoot, all expenses paid. We'll cover travel, accommodations, everything."

This was it. The opportunity he'd been waiting for. The chance to take his career to the next level. But before he could start mentally packing his bags, Marcy hit him with the kicker.

"It's scheduled for Christmas Day, you're light leaves at 9 pm tonight."

Demetri's stomach dropped. Of course it was. Why wouldn't it be?

"Christmas Day?" he echoed, his voice strained.

"I know it's short notice," Marcy continued, "but this could be huge for you. We're talking national exposure. Magazine spreads. Online features. This could be the break you've been waiting for."

Demetri closed his eyes, the weight of the decision pressing down on him. He could already hear Monique's voice in his head, reminding him of all the holidays and birthdays he'd missed. King's disappointed face flashed through his mind. He'd promised them both that this Christmas would be different since he spent the last 3 Christmas holidays working.

But then he thought about the hundred grand he owed the IRS. The looming threat of financial ruin. This job could be his way out of that hole.

"I need to think about it," he said, his voice barely above a whisper.

"Demetri, I understand, but they need an answer by the end of the day. If you don't take this, they'll have to move on to the next photographer."

The end of the day. That didn't give him much time. He was already behind on his errands, not to mention the fact that he hadn't even started Christmas shopping for King. Could he really afford to turn this down?

"Fine," he said after a long pause. "I'll let you know by tonight."

"Perfect! I'll be waiting for your call." Marcy hung up, leaving Demetri staring at the phone in his hand like it was a ticking time bomb.

"What was that about?" Sharon asked, her arms still crossed as she watched him.

"An offer," Demetri muttered, still processing everything. "A big one. A Christmas Day shoot with Bureau Luxe."

"Christmas Day?" Sharon's eyebrows shot up. "But you promised King you'd be there this year."

"I know." Demetri ran a hand through his hair, frustration bubbling up inside him. "But this could fix everything. The IRS. The money. I could pay off my debt."

Sharon stared at him for a long moment, then sighed. "You need to figure out what's more important, Demetri. Your career... or your family."

She was right, of course. But that didn't make the decision any easier.

Without another word, Demetri grabbed his jacket and headed for the door. He needed to get out of the office, clear his head. Maybe pick up a few Christmas presents for King. If he could still access his credit cards, that was.

"Where are you going?" Sharon called after him.

"To do some last-minute shopping," he replied over his shoulder. "And to figure out what the hell I'm going to do."

The streets of Shreveport were a madhouse.

Demetri weaved through traffic, his eyes darting between the road and the holiday shoppers clogging the sidewalks. The radio went on about the biggest snowfall Shreveport had seen in years was on its way. He hadn't realized just how late it had gotten, and the Christmas rush was in full swing. Cars honked impatiently as people tried to find parking, while pedestrians shuffled along with armfuls of bags and boxes, hurrying from one store to the next.

As he approached the mall, Demetri's stomach twisted. He hadn't even thought about what to get King this year. All he knew was that his son had been hinting about a basketball jersey—something special, from his favorite team—but Demetri had been so wrapped up in work that he'd completely forgotten to pick it up.

"Damn it," he muttered, gripping the steering wheel tighter. His mind raced as he tried to come up with a plan. A car horn blared, snapping him out of his thoughts just as a pedestrian stepped off the curb in front of him. Demetri slammed on the brakes, narrowly avoiding the man, who shot him a dirty look as he hurried across the street.

"Sorry!" Demetri called through the window, but the man was already gone, lost in the sea of shoppers.

He couldn't keep doing this—juggling work, money, family, all while trying to hold everything together. Something had to give. And soon.

But right now, all he could think about was getting through the next few hours. The idea of pulling up to King's school with nothing for Christmas gnawed at his conscience. He could already picture the look of disappointment in his son's eyes, the silent accusation that his father had let him down once again.

Demetri pulled into the mall's parking lot, and, of course, it was packed. Cars circled like vultures, waiting for any spot to open. His heart raced as he glanced at the time—he only had a couple of hours to make this right. **King** would be out of school soon, and he needed to have something—anything under the tree—that would show he'd at least tried.

After several frustrating minutes, he finally spotted someone backing out of a spot. Demetri swerved in, narrowly beating out another driver. He gave a quick wave, half an apology, before jumping out of the car and jogging toward the mall entrance. The cold air stung his face, but he barely felt it. His mind was elsewhere.

Inside, the mall was even worse. People moved in packs, zig-zagging between stores, their arms loaded with bags. Christmas music blared from the speakers, jolly and incessant, as if mocking his growing sense of panic. He quickly scanned the directory, trying to figure out where the sports shop was. King had mentioned something about a special edition jersey, and he was determined to find it.

He went to the ATM and tried to pull out cash in case the jersey was sold out, he would have the cash needed to buy it off someone. "Insufficient Funds" the screen read. "What the?" he quickly texted Sharon 'what was the date from the IRS letter' she texted back '3 months ago'. Demetri stomach dropped as he glanced at the last jersey on the rack. And now, with his accounts frozen, he wasn't sure how he was going to pay for it. He reached for his phone, scrolling through his banking app, hoping there was some mistake, some glitch that would miraculously unfreeze his funds.

No such luck.

As he started toward the escalator, his phone buzzed in his pocket again. He pulled it out and saw Sharon's name flashing on the screen. He almost ignored it—he didn't have time to deal with another crisis right now—but something told him to pick up.

"Sharon, I'm in the middle of something," he said as he dodged a group of teenagers taking selfies by a giant Christmas tree.

"Demetri, I'm sorry to bother you, but you've got another problem," Sharon said, her tone urgent.

He paused, heart sinking. "What now?"

"I just got off the phone with your bank," she continued. "It's not just your personal accounts that are frozen. It's your business ones too. They've locked everything down."

Demetri stopped dead in his tracks, the noise of the mall fading into the background as her words sank in. "What do you mean everything?"

"Everything, Demetri. Your credit lines, your savings, your business account—it's all been frozen. Apparently, you've missed more than just your tax payments."

He felt like the floor was falling out from under him. "Sharon, I can't—" He swallowed hard, his voice shaking. "I can't pay for anything right now. Not even for King's Christmas presents."

"I know," she said softly. "And I'm sorry, but you've got to figure this out before it gets worse. You have to decide about that Bureau Luxe shoot. It could be your ticket out of this mess."

Demetri's chest tightened, and for a moment, he couldn't breathe. Sharon's words echoed in his head: **Your ticket out of this mess**. It was tempting. So tempting. But the thought of missing another Christmas with his son twisted his stomach in knots.

"I'll... I'll call you back," he managed, hanging up before she could say anything else.

The mall buzzed around him, oblivious to his personal crisis. People were laughing, exchanging gifts, taking pictures with Santa. And there he was, standing in the middle of it all, paralyzed by indecision. On one hand, he could take the job, pay off his debt, and salvage his career. On the other, he could spend Christmas with King, as he'd promised, and try—once again—to make up for all the times he hadn't been there.

His eyes darted to a nearby sports store, the one that sold the jerseys King had been talking about for weeks. He knew it wasn't about the jersey—it was about being there. About showing up, proving that he cared.

But how could he do that when everything was falling apart?

With a deep breath, Demetri pushed forward, weaving through the crowds until he reached the store. The shelves were lined with jerseys, sneakers, basketballs, and everything else King loved. He moved to the section that housed the team King adored, and after a few moments of searching, he found it—the limited-edition jersey King had been raving about.

A tiny flicker of hope sparked in Demetri's chest as he pulled the jersey off the rack. Maybe this was it. Maybe this would make things okay. He walked to the register, ignoring the gnawing anxiety in the pit of his stomach as he handed the jersey to the cashier.

"That'll be $349.99," the cashier said, ringing up the item with a cheery smile.

Demetri pulled out his credit card and swiped it through the reader. The machine beeped, and a red message flashed across the screen.

DECLINED.

His heart sank as the cashier looked up at him with a sympathetic smile. "I'm sorry, sir. It's been declined."

He tried again. Same result.

Panic clawed at his chest. This couldn't be happening. Not now. Not when he was so close.

"I think there's a mistake," Demetri stammered, pulling out another card and swiping it. But deep down, he already knew the truth.

DECLINED.

He stared at the cashier, the reality of his situation crashing down on him. His accounts were frozen. He had no way of paying for anything.

"Sir?" the cashier said gently. "Do you have another form of payment?"

Demetri's mouth went dry. He could feel the eyes of the people behind him in line, the awkward tension of the moment thick in the air. "Uh... no. No, I don't."

The cashier gave him an understanding nod as she slid the jersey back across the counter. "I'm sorry."

Demetri muttered something unintelligible and turned to leave, his face burning with embarrassment. He felt like a failure. No, he *was* a failure. He couldn't even buy his son a Christmas gift.

As he stepped out of the store, his phone buzzed again. This time, he didn't need to look to know who it was.

Marcy.

He stood there, staring at his phone, torn between answering the call and tossing it into the nearest trash can. He knew what she was going to say. The same thing Sharon had said. **This job could save you**. And they were right. It could. But at what cost?

With a heavy sigh, he answered the call. "Marcy."

"Demetri! Glad I caught you. Listen, I'm going to need an answer soon. The team at Bureau Luxe is waiting, and if we don't get confirmation by the end of the day, we'll have to go with someone else."

Demetri's throat tightened. He could picture King's face—how his eyes would light up when he saw the jersey, how he'd smile when Demetri finally showed up for Christmas, just like he'd promised. But he could also picture the IRS breathing down his neck, his accounts frozen, his career slipping through his fingers.

"I... I need more time," he said, though he knew it wasn't the answer she wanted.

"I wish I could give you more time, Demetri, but we're on a deadline here. If you want this, you need to commit. Now."

His heart pounded in his chest as he stood there, torn between the two worlds that were pulling him apart. He knew what he *should* do. But knowing and doing were two very different things.

"I'll call you back," he said quickly, hanging up before she could press him further.

For a long moment, he stood there in the middle of the crowded mall, feeling completely and utterly lost. The Christmas lights twinkled overhead, and the sound of carolers filled the air, but all Demetri could think about was how everything had gone so wrong.

He had a decision to make. And no matter what he chose, he knew he'd be letting someone down. Demetri's legs felt heavy as he moved through the throngs of holiday shoppers, his steps slow and unsure. The weight of the decisions ahead of him—career or family, money or love—clung to him like the biting December air. The twinkling lights around him, meant to symbolize hope and cheer, now felt like a cruel reminder of how tangled his life had become.

He walked aimlessly for a while, weaving through crowds of families who seemed blissfully unaware of the struggles gnawing at him. Every child clutching a new toy or eagerly tugging at a parent's hand toward another store reminded him of King and the countless promises he had failed to keep.

Finally, he stopped near the food court, leaning against a pillar as the bustling holiday crowd swarmed around him. His phone buzzed again in his pocket. This time, it was a text from **Monique**.

Monique: Don't forget to pick King game at 12, we're on our way now. And I hope you went to Christmas already. He's looking forward to that jersey.

Demetri stared at the message for a moment "How can I forget that he out of school for winter break, and how could I forget about the game today, his heart sinking deeper into his chest. She didn't even have to say anything else. He could read between the lines. Monique had long given up on expecting him to show up for anything. She was trying, for King's sake, to be civil, but he knew the disappointment in her voice even before she typed it out. **She didn't believe him**—and worse, King probably didn't either.

He glanced at his watch. It was almost 11:30. He needed to get his son's game soon, but the pressing weight of the decision he had to make loomed over him like a dark cloud.

For a fleeting moment, he considered calling Monique, telling her about the job, the IRS, and the stress he'd been buried under. But what would that accomplish? An apology? An excuse? Another promise he wasn't sure he could keep?

With a deep sigh, he shoved the phone back into his pocket. He needed to make a decision, and soon. The words of both Sharon and Marcy echoed in his head. **This could save you.** But at what cost?

He stood up straight, glancing at the directory. He had no money for presents, no way to fix the mess he'd created—not without the job. The realization hit him harder than he expected. **He needed to take it.** He hated the thought of missing another Christmas with King, but what good was he as a father if they ended up broke and drowning in debt?

Pushing through the growing sense of dread, Demetri headed back toward the parking lot. If he was going to get through the day, he had to make this decision—one way or another. At the very least, he'd make it to King's game, try to salvage what was left of the day, and then figure out what the hell he was going to do about the Bureau Luxe offer.

But as soon as he reached his car and slid into the driver's seat, a knock banged against the window. It was **Cam**.

Demetri hesitated. He hadn't spoken to his cousin in months, and the last time they'd talked, it had been about a "business opportunity" that Demetri had wisely opted out of. Cam was trouble, plain and simple—always chasing the next scheme, always looking for a quick score. Demetri wasn't in the mood for whatever mess Cam had gotten himself into now.

But something made him open the door anyway.

"Cam," Demetri said, his voice wary. "What do you want?"

"D! Man, I'm glad you picked me up jumping into the passenger seat wearing a fast food uniform. I'm in a bit of a situation," Cam's voice shaking, laced with the kind of desperation that only Cam could muster. "I need a favor."

Demetri rubbed his temple, his patience already wearing thin. "I'm kind of in the middle of something, Cam. I got this big list of Christmas gifts and the mall is all out," flashing his Christmas list that Sharon had for him a month ago.

"No, no, hear me out. I've got this deal—seriously, it's a quick thing—and it could solve a lot of your problems. You still need Christmas gifts for King, right?"

Demetri froze, his grip on the steering wheel tightening. "I just said that, how did you even know I was here?"

" You always forget to turn off your location sharing, bro. Don't worry, I'm not stalking you, but I knew you'd be out shopping last minute, like you always do. Look, I can hook you up."

Demetri's skepticism grew. "What's the catch, Cam?"

"No catch! Okay, maybe a small catch. You remember Lil Tone?"

Demetri groaned inwardly. Of course, Lil Tone was involved. The guy was bad news from the start—always skirting the law, always looking for the next illegal way to make a quick buck. And somehow, Cam had ended up in his orbit.

"Cam, I told you, I'm not getting involved in whatever you and Lil Tone are up to. I don't need more trouble in my life."

"Hey, I'm not asking for anything crazy, okay?" Cam said quickly. "Look, I know you've got bills to pay. I know about the IRS thing. I've got a way for you to get what you need for King, and maybe even some extra cash."

Demetri's breath caught in his throat. How did Cam know about the IRS? Did Sharon mention it? Or was he just that transparent these days?

"I don't have time for this, Cam."

"Look, man, I'm serious. I can get you everything on King's list. All brand new stuff. No strings attached. Just help me out with this one thing, and we're square."

Demetri squeezed the bridge of his nose, the pounding in his head growing louder. "And what's the 'one thing,' Cam? Because I know it's not as simple as you're making it sound."

Cam chuckled, a nervous edge to his voice. "Just bring me to the alley behind Fletcher's. I'll explain everything when you get here."

"Fletcher's?" Demetri frowned, recognizing the name of the rundown pawn shop Cam had always frequented. It was never a good sign when Cam asked him to go there. "You better not be dragging me into some shady shit."

"Relax, D. It's nothing major. Just trust me, alright?"

Demetri wasn't sure if he'd ever trusted Cam—not fully. But right now, he was desperate. And desperate men did desperate things. Against his better judgment, he agreed.

"Fine. Let's go."

Chapter 2: Missed Promises and New Tension

The high-pitched squeal of sneakers against polished wood echoed through the local gymnasium as the basketball hit the rim and bounced off. The buzzer rang out, signaling the end of the game. King, drenched in sweat, wiped his forehead with his arm, glancing up at the scoreboard. His team had won by two points, and his teammates rushed past him, high-fiving one another and celebrating their victory.

But King didn't join in.

Instead, he scanned the bleachers, looking for one face in particular. His heart sank when he didn't see his father. He had been sure, just this once, Demetri would show up. King's mom, Monique, sat in her usual spot near the front, clapping and smiling, but the empty seat next to her was glaringly obvious.

"Good game, kiddo!" one of the dads called out, ruffling King's hair as he passed by.

King gave a small nod but barely acknowledged him. He threw his towel over his shoulder and walked slowly toward the sideline, feeling every bit of the weight of his father's absence.

Monique's smile faded as she saw her son's expression. She knew exactly what was going through his mind. How many times had Demetri promised he'd make it to a game? How many times had he let them both down?

"You played great, King," she said as he approached, bending down to look him in the eyes. She pulled a water bottle from her bag and handed it to him.

"Thanks, Mom." King's voice was flat, lacking the usual energy he had after a win.

Monique sighed, brushing her hand over his hair. "I know you're disappointed... but your dad's really trying."

King didn't respond. Instead, he just shrugged and took a long drink from the water bottle. He hated hearing the same excuses, the same promises that never seemed to pan out.

"Are we going home?" he asked, eager to leave the gymnasium and avoid talking about his dad any longer.

illegal way to make a quick buck. And somehow, Cam had ended up in his orbit.

"Cam, I told you, I'm not getting involved in whatever you and Lil Tone are up to. I don't need more trouble in my life."

"Hey, I'm not asking for anything crazy, okay?" Cam said quickly. "Look, I know you've got bills to pay. I know about the IRS thing. I've got a way for you to get what you need for King, and maybe even some extra cash."

Demetri's breath caught in his throat. How did Cam know about the IRS? Did Sharon mention it? Or was he just that transparent these days?

"I don't have time for this, Cam."

"Look, man, I'm serious. I can get you everything on King's list. All brand new stuff. No strings attached. Just help me out with this one thing, and we're square."

Demetri squeezed the bridge of his nose, the pounding in his head growing louder. "And what's the 'one thing,' Cam? Because I know it's not as simple as you're making it sound."

Cam chuckled, a nervous edge to his voice. "Just bring me to the alley behind Fletcher's. I'll explain everything when you get here."

"Fletcher's?" Demetri frowned, recognizing the name of the rundown pawn shop Cam had always frequented. It was never a good sign when Cam asked him to go there. "You better not be dragging me into some shady shit."

"Relax, D. It's nothing major. Just trust me, alright?"

Demetri wasn't sure if he'd ever trusted Cam—not fully. But right now, he was desperate. And desperate men did desperate things. Against his better judgment, he agreed.

"Fine. Let's go."

Chapter 2: Missed Promises and New Tension

The high-pitched squeal of sneakers against polished wood echoed through the local gymnasium as the basketball hit the rim and bounced off. The buzzer rang out, signaling the end of the game. King, drenched in sweat, wiped his forehead with his arm, glancing up at the scoreboard. His team had won by two points, and his teammates rushed past him, high-fiving one another and celebrating their victory.

But King didn't join in.

Instead, he scanned the bleachers, looking for one face in particular. His heart sank when he didn't see his father. He had been sure, just this once, Demetri would show up. King's mom, Monique, sat in her usual spot near the front, clapping and smiling, but the empty seat next to her was glaringly obvious.

"Good game, kiddo!" one of the dads called out, ruffling King's hair as he passed by.

King gave a small nod but barely acknowledged him. He threw his towel over his shoulder and walked slowly toward the sideline, feeling every bit of the weight of his father's absence.

Monique's smile faded as she saw her son's expression. She knew exactly what was going through his mind. How many times had Demetri promised he'd make it to a game? How many times had he let them both down?

"You played great, King," she said as he approached, bending down to look him in the eyes. She pulled a water bottle from her bag and handed it to him.

"Thanks, Mom." King's voice was flat, lacking the usual energy he had after a win.

Monique sighed, brushing her hand over his hair. "I know you're disappointed... but your dad's really trying."

King didn't respond. Instead, he just shrugged and took a long drink from the water bottle. He hated hearing the same excuses, the same promises that never seemed to pan out.

"Are we going home?" he asked, eager to leave the gymnasium and avoid talking about his dad any longer.

"We need to make a quick stop first," Monique replied, grabbing her bag and motioning toward the exit. "We're out of groceries for Christmas dinner, and I need to pick up a few things."

King nodded reluctantly, and the two made their way out of the gym. Monique could feel the tension hanging between them, a mixture of disappointment and frustration that had become all too familiar in their family. She hated how much it affected King, but she didn't know what else to say. Demetri's absence spoke louder than any excuse she could come up with.

Outside the store, the scene was chaotic. Shoppers hurried in and out, arms laden with bags, while holiday decorations blinked above their heads in a dizzying array of colors. Amidst the mayhem stood a skinny man in the parking lot, nearly swallowed by an oversized Santa suit that looked like it had seen better days. The fake fur trim was patchy, and the black boots—at least three sizes too big—slapped the pavement as he shuffled in place, trying to get people's attention.

In his hands, he held a stack of what looked like credit cards, only they were glittery and had the words "Black Assets" scrawled across them in sharpie. The oversized Santa swayed from side to side, waving one of the cards like a baton as he eyed the incoming shoppers. He had clearly found his next target.

"Black assets!" he yelled, his voice hoarse but enthusiastic. "We all need 'em! Let Black Santa get you hooked up this holiday season!"

Monique and King approached, Monique steering the cart with one hand and holding King's hand with the other. She had just about had it with the day. Between Demetri's absence at the game and King's mood, she was running on fumes. But this Black Santa wasn't done yet.

"Excuse me, ma'am! Ma'am!" Black Santa hollered, shuffling closer with a strange hop-step like his shoes were filled with rocks. "You know you need some assets, let Santa drop off some holiday cheer!"

Monique glanced at him for a moment before quickly looking away, pulling King closer to her side. She wasn't about to let herself get roped into whatever nonsense this was.

"Ma'am, don't walk away from a blessing!" Black Santa bellowed, moving in a little closer, now half-jogging to keep up. "Bitcoin is the future! I got your financial freedom right here." He wagged a shiny card in front of them, grinning widely.

Monique picked up the pace, her heels clicking a little louder on the pavement. King looked up at her, his face caught between confusion and amusement. "Mom, what's he talking about?" King asked, trying to stifle a laugh.

"Nothing, King. Just keep walking," Monique muttered under her breath, tugging him along faster.

But Black Santa wasn't giving up that easily. "Ma'am! Ma'am! Wait! You're gonna regret this. Black Santa's here to help you with those holiday expenses!" He waved his arms theatrically, almost slipping on a stray patch of ice, which only made him flail harder.

"Don't you want to be part of the future?" he continued, his voice rising in desperation as they approached their car. "Black Assets—straight to the moon, baby! Let me bless your financial portfolio! I got cards, I got crypto. I even got a discount if you buy two! What's Santa gotta do to help you get those holiday gains?"

"Okay, okay, listen. This one's on the house, just 'cause I'm in the holiday spirit," he wheezed, out of breath from his relentless pursuit. "One free Black Asset, no strings attached! You can't beat that. You'll be thanking me this time next year when you're sitting on a stack of crypto taller than your Christmas tree."

Monique turned to him, her patience finally snapping. "Look, I appreciate the... enthusiasm. But I'm good. We're all good here."

"Just remember, Santa tried to bless you today. Don't say I never did nothing for you!" he said, tapping his nose and then attempting to waddle away in the oversized boots. One step, two steps, and—BAM—he tripped on a loose shoelace, sprawling out face-first onto the sidewalk.

Monique winced as she watched him try to pull himself up, the big fake Santa beard twisted around his head like a noose.

"Mom, do you think he's okay?" King asked, holding back laughter.

Monique shook her head, hiding a grin. "Yeah, King. I'm sure he'll be fine. But we're definitely not getting any 'Black Assets' today." She stormed into the store.

As she entered, they could still hear Black Santa calling after them, his voice fading into the background.

"You'll regret it! Straight to the moon!"

The grocery store was packed, filled with last-minute shoppers bustling through the aisles, carts overflowing with holiday foods. Monique grabbed a cart as she and King entered the store, mentally running through her shopping list. She didn't need much, just the basics to round out their Christmas meal. Ham, potatoes, stuffing... nothing extravagant, but enough to make it feel like Christmas.

Monique turned down the cereal aisle, only to find herself face-to-face with a chaotic, post-apocalyptic scene—half the shelves were bare, and two moms were in a silent standoff over the last turkey. One woman had her hand on the box, the other had already wedged her cart in front of it.

"Ma'am, I touched it first," the first mom said, narrowing her eyes.

"You touched it, but did you *claim* it?" the other shot back, leaning over her cart as if she were ready to block a rebound.

Monique couldn't help but smirk as she watched the showdown, pushing King forward as he absentmindedly bumped into a display of gingerbread houses. The whole thing tumbled like a sugary avalanche.

"Sorry!" King mumbled, quickly picking up a fallen roof piece and trying to fix the house before anyone noticed.

Monique sighed, shaking her head. "C'mon, King, let's grab the ham before things really go south around here."

Just as they started to move forward, a man in a reindeer onesie skidded by, pushing a shopping cart filled only with eggnog and candy canes. He waved cheerily at Monique.

"Stock up before Santa cleans us out!" he yelled before crashing into a tower of canned cranberry sauce.

Monique blinked, biting back a laugh. "Okay... let's speed this up before we get caught in a food fight."

King's lips quirked up just slightly, and Monique considered that a win.

As they made their way through the crowded store, King trailed behind her, his head down. He wasn't paying much attention, his thoughts still lingering on the empty seat at his game.

"**Hey, Monique!**"

Monique turned at the familiar voice and immediately felt an internal groan rise in her chest. There, blocking her path to the frozen turkeys, stood Coach Moonie, King's overly enthusiastic basketball coach. He was wearing what could only be described as an offensively bright Christmas sweater, complete with blinking lights, a reindeer, and what looked suspiciously like a miniature wreath hanging from the collar. His grin stretched from ear to ear, as though he was the living embodiment of holiday cheer—except Monique wasn't feeling particularly cheery.

"Monique!" Moonie beamed, pushing his cart forward with the enthusiasm of someone who'd just discovered Christmas for the first time. "Just the woman I was hoping to see today!"

Monique tried to keep her smile polite, but it was strained at best. "Hey, Coach. Fancy meeting you here." She glanced at King, who gave Moonie a look that said *oh great, this guy again*.

Moonie didn't seem to notice King's expression—or if he did, he was doing a great job of pretending he didn't. "Just picking up some last-minute groceries myself," he said, gesturing to his cart, which contained nothing but an army of eggnog cartons and what looked like a single box of instant mashed potatoes.

Monique's eyebrows shot up. "Big meal planned?"

"Oh, you know," Moonie winked, "just keeping it simple this year."

"Clearly," Monique muttered under her breath, but loud enough that King snickered beside her.

Moonie bent down slightly to meet King's eyes. "Hey there, champ! You played a hell of a game today. You're going to be a star, no doubt about it."

King gave him a tight-lipped smile that had all the enthusiasm of a kid forced to eat broccoli. "Thanks, Coach," he muttered, looking like he'd rather be anywhere else.

Before Monique could steer the conversation elsewhere, Moonie's eyes darted to her half-full cart. "Need any help with those groceries? You look like you've got your hands full."

Monique's instinct was to politely decline, but before she could get a word out, Moonie had already plucked a couple of items from the cart, including a box of stuffing and a ham that he held up like a trophy. "Let me lighten your load."

"Really, it's fine," Monique insisted, trying to keep the tension out of her voice. But Moonie, oblivious as ever, sidled up next to her, throwing on his best "helpful guy" face.

"The holidays are stressful, Monique. You don't need to be doing this all by yourself," he said, inching closer in a way that made Monique's skin crawl.

King's eyebrows furrowed, his lips pressing into a thin line. "We're good, Coach," he said, his tone sharp.

Moonie chuckled, completely undeterred by the boy's tone. "Just trying to help out where I can. A woman like you shouldn't be handling all this by herself."

There it was. That undercurrent Monique had been dreading, the not-so-subtle implication in his voice. She tried to keep her cool, though her grip tightened on the cart. "I manage just fine, but thanks for the concern," she said with a forced smile.

Moonie leaned in slightly, lowering his voice as if he were telling her a secret. "You know, Monique, if you ever need someone to talk to or... help with anything, I'm just a call away."

Monique's smile froze in place. "That's kind of you, but really—"

"We don't need anything," King interrupted, stepping in front of his mother as if Moonie were about to steal their groceries. His tone was firm, and for a moment, Monique was taken aback by how protective he sounded. "We're fine."

Moonie blinked, seemingly caught off guard by King's sudden boldness. He raised his hands in mock surrender, the blinking lights on his sweater adding an unintentional level of absurdity to the moment. "Alright, alright, champ. Just trying to spread some holiday cheer."

Monique gave King a small, grateful nod as they moved toward the checkout lane. Moonie, still undeterred, followed closely behind, casually dropping, "You know, Monique, a little gratitude goes a long way. You never know when someone might need a favor in return." He flashed what he likely thought was a disarming grin.

At the register, Monique began pulling out her wallet, but Moonie swooped in, producing his credit card with a flourish. "Let me take care of this. I insist."

"Oh, really, you don't have to do that," Monique protested, but Moonie was already handing his card to the cashier.

"Nonsense! It's the season of giving, after all," he said, puffing out his chest like he'd just saved Christmas single-handedly. "Consider it a little Christmas gift from me to you."

Monique gave him a tight-lipped smile, ready to get out of there. As they walked toward the exit, Moonie still carrying a couple of bags despite her earlier refusals, King shot him a glare that could've melted snow.

"I'll just help you to the car," Moonie said, as if he hadn't been told *no* three times already.

But King wasn't having it. He stepped forward, snatching the bags from Moonie's hands. "We got it, Coach," he said, the words clipped and final.

Moonie's smile faltered for the briefest of moments, but then he plastered it back on, nodding like he hadn't just been shooed off by a nine-year-old. "Alright, champ. See you at the next game," he said, giving them a little wave as they finally made their way to the parking lot.

Once they were safely in the car, Monique exhaled a long breath. King crossed his arms, his brows still furrowed. "What's with him?"

Monique shook her head, gripping the steering wheel a little tighter. "He's just... friendly."

King snorted. "Friendly's one word for it."

Monique couldn't help but laugh. "Don't worry about him, King. He's harmless."

King looked out the window, unconvinced. "Still weird. I don't like it."

Monique glanced at her son and smiled softly. "Me neither, kiddo."

Monique's fingers clenched the steering wheel as she watched the dashboard lights blink wildly. The grocery bags rustled in the backseat, jostling with every turn. King sat beside her, his head resting against the window, staring out at the rows of twinkling holiday lights illuminating the grocery store parking lot. The engine sputtered before coughing to a dead halt, leaving the car eerily silent.

"Not now... come on," Monique muttered under her breath, as she turned the key again. The engine responded with nothing but a weak whirr.

King lifted his head. "What's wrong with the car?"

King stepped out of the car and peered at the headlights, noticing a faint flicker. "I think you left the lights on, Mom," he said, pointing. Monique groaned as she unbuckled her seatbelt and stepped out into the cold night air. She popped the hood and stared blankly at the engine. She had no idea what she was looking for, and the sight of the cold metal only made her feel more helpless. With a frustrated sigh, she slammed it shut and hurried back into the warmth of the car.

Just as she was settling back into her seat, her phone buzzed. She glanced at the screen and rolled her eyes. Demetri. The nerve.

She answered it, cutting him off before he could even get a word out. "I don't want to hear it," Monique snapped, her breath fogging up the chilly car window. King sat beside her, huddled up in his jacket, watching quietly. "You promised King you'd be at his game, Demetri. Again. And guess what? You never showed."

Demetri sat at home, packing a suitcase, the phone pressed to his ear as his face flushed with guilt. He motioned for Cam, who was busy rifling through his things, to be quiet. "Babe, listen—just hear me out," Demetri pleaded.

Monique scoffed, shaking her head in disbelief. "Hear you out? For what? Another excuse?"

Demetri swallowed hard, his eyes darting around the room, searching for the right words. "I've got a job offer, Monique. Six figures for one shoot. This could change everything for us. I'm talking about gifts for King, a better car for you—no more broken-down nights like this."

"When?" Monique asked flatly, already bracing herself for the answer.

"Christmas Day," he admitted, his voice soft, knowing how bad it sounded. He waited for the explosion.

Monique sighed deeply, her frustration mounting. "Christmas Day. Of course." She leaned back, rubbing her temple as snowflakes began to softly land on the windshield. "Demetri, I'm sitting in a dead car with ten bags of groceries. It's freezing. I'm tired. I can't keep doing this by myself."

Her words hit him like a punch to the gut. "What are you saying?" Demetri whispered.

"I'm saying I'm done, Demetri. I'm tired. And so is King," Monique's voice cracked slightly as the weight of it all pressed down on her. She glanced at King, who was staring at the snow outside, pretending not to listen.

"I just want to give King what I didn't have," Demetri said quietly, his voice desperate now. "You know my dad wasn't around. I'm trying to be better for him."

Monique's heart ached at those words, but she couldn't let them soften her resolve. "Being there doesn't mean just buying things, Demetri. It means showing up. It means being present."

There was a long, heavy silence on both ends of the line. Finally, Monique shook her head, her voice soft but firm. "Bye, Demetri." She hung up, the sound of the call ending echoing in the quiet car.

Monique sighed again, resting her head against the seat, her eyes closing as the exhaustion of the day threatened to overwhelm her. "I don't know, King," she said quietly, more to herself than to him. "I really don't know what to do."

King turned to her, his young face showing a wisdom beyond his years. "It's okay, Mom. We'll figure it out."

Chapter 3: Car Trouble and Dark Deals

Just as Monique was about to call a tow truck, a sharp knock on the window made both of them jump. Monique looked up to see Coach Moonie's grinning face peering in, his Christmas sweater blinking like a neon billboard. She groaned inwardly. Of all people to show up now.

Monique rolled the window down just a crack, enough to speak through. "Hey, Coach," she said, trying to sound polite despite the exhaustion.

"Everything alright?" Moonie asked, his grin still plastered on his face. His eyes darted between her and King.

Monique sighed, glancing back at King before answering. "Car won't start."

Moonie's grin widened, as if this were a golden opportunity. "No problem! I'll give you two a ride home."

Monique hesitated. There was something about his over-eagerness that set off alarm bells. She looked over at King, who was already narrowing his eyes at Moonie's familiar enthusiasm. "Really, Coach, we're fine," Monique said, hoping he'd take the hint.

"Nonsense!" Moonie laughed, already making his way toward his truck, which was parked a few spots down. "No one should be stuck out here in the cold, especially not on Christmas Eve. Let me help."

Monique clenched her jaw, but reality was hitting her hard. She was tired, cold, and stuck in a parking lot at night. Her better judgment told her to decline, but practicality forced her to reconsider. She exchanged a look with King, who just shrugged, clearly unhappy but also understanding the situation.

"Okay, but just a ride home," Monique finally relented, her voice firm.

Moonie's grin stretched even wider as he ushered them toward his truck. "Of course, of course! I'd be a terrible coach if I didn't help out my star player and his wonderful mom!"

King climbed out of the car first, eyeing Moonie suspiciously as he grabbed some of the grocery bags. Monique followed, reluctantly allowing Moonie to take more than his share of bags. The ride home was awkwardly quiet. Moonie hummed along to the Christmas music on the radio, making light conversation about the basketball game, but Monique wasn't in the mood. She just wanted to get home.

King, on the other hand, sat in the back seat, arms crossed and staring out the window as the snow began to fall heavily. He wasn't buying Moonie's cheerful act and made sure to keep a close eye on him. The radio warned of roads closing as the snowstorm approached.

As Demetri and Cam navigated the slick, icy roads, the snow kept falling in thick flurries. Demetri gripped the wheel tight, his knuckles turning white, eyes darting between the road and his cousin, who was acting way too jumpy for his liking. Cam was rubbing his hands together, eyes flicking back and forth like he was expecting the cops to swoop down on them any minute.

Demetri raised an eyebrow, side-eyeing him with a frown. "Yo, what's been going on with you?"

Cam broke into a wide, almost manic grin. "Man, I just got out the pen today."

Demetri shot him a sideways glance, taking in the wrinkled Burger King uniform that didn't quite fit. "In a Burger King uniform?" He shook his head in disbelief. "I thought you said you were done with that dumb stuff?"

"I am, I am," Cam said quickly, nodding like a bobblehead. "But listen, this ain't even like that. So, peep game. I DM this chick, right? Her relationship status says engaged, but she tells me it's just a front."

Demetri's face scrunched up in confusion. "A front? What, like a cover-up?"

"Exactly!" Cam's eyes lit up, and he leaned forward, clearly excited to share this ridiculous tale. "So I'm like, cool, no problem, right? I head to her spot, we chillin', things heat up, and we in the bed. Everything smooth as butter. Then boom, somebody knocks on the door."

Demetri, against his better judgment, was already invested. "Oh, hell. Then what?"

Cam rubbed his hands together like he was telling a ghost story. "So I'm thinking, who the hell is that? Next thing I know, this big ol' dude walks in—300 pounds of pure muscle. He like a human bulldozer. Now, at this point, I'm butt naked, right?"

Demetri groaned, already regretting asking. "Aw man, I don't wanna hear this—"

"Nah, nah, wait for it!" Cam's voice shot up a pitch. "I'm thinking I'm done for, bro. But then I notice... the dude is blind. BLIND! So I'm like, whew,

I'm good! But then this fool starts stripping! He's takin' his clothes off, all slow-motion-like, like he about to hop in the bed with me!"

Demetri shot Cam a wide-eyed look, half horrified, half cracking up. "Wait, WHAT?"

Cam nodded dramatically. "Yes, bruh! Next thing you know, I'm stuck under him! I'm squished like a damn pancake! He's rolling around, and I'm yelling like, 'I DON'T PLAY THAT!' I drop to the floor, commando-style, crawling outta there like it's a war zone. This dude is swinging in the air like he trying to hit Trey from *Boyz n the Hood*, just missing everything!"

Demetri clamped his hand over his mouth, trying not to laugh. "You're lying!"

"I swear!" Cam insisted. "And the girl? Man, she's nowhere to be found! So I'm like, forget this, I gotta make my escape. I look up, and I see her about to jump out the window. I'm like, 'HELL NAW, I'M COMING TOO!' So we both jump out that window, butt naked, looking like two wild hyenas running through the damn jungle. We running down the street, jingle bells swinging in the wind!"

At this point, Demetri was shaking with laughter, tears welling up in his eyes. "Yo, that's WILD, man. So what happened next?"

Cam slapped his knee. "Man, we run for like two blocks, bare as the day we were born, and then a car pulls up. Dude rolls the window down all smooth, and he's like, 'Baby, get in.' I'm like, 'Who the hell is this?' And she's like, 'Oh, that's my fiancé.'"

Demetri's laughter died in his throat. "Wait, WHAT?!"

"Right! I'm like, 'Yo, then WHOSE HOUSE were we in?!'" Cam threw his hands up dramatically. "Man, I turn the corner, tryin' to get away, and BAM! I run face-first into the window of a damn donut shop. Turns out, it's free donut day, and the place is packed... with COPS. Whole squad in there, just munching away.

They all turn and look at me like I'm the glazed special. Before I know it, I'm cuffed for indecent exposure!"

Demetri finally lost it, laughing so hard he could barely keep the car on the road. "Man, you're a whole mess, you know that?"

Cam shrugged, grinning. "Hey, at least I got out. Now I just gotta avoid blind bodybuilders for the rest of my life."

Demetri shook his head, still chuckling as he navigated the icy road. "You're unbelievable."

The snow was coming down harder now, swirling through the air like confetti in a blizzard. Officers had set up roadblocks to close off certain streets, and Moonie, always full of energy, was now standing outside his truck with a handful of soul and gospel CDs. He fanned them out like a magician revealing a trick. "Alright, Monique, I've got Chaka Khan, Teddy Pendergrass, Luther Vandross, and—oh look—Charles Jenkins. Go ahead, take your pick."

Monique gave him a polite smile, flipping through the CD collection, more out of courtesy than interest. "Hmm, gotta go with Teddy," she said, pulling out a CD. "And 'By God is Awesome' by Charles Jenkins. That's my favorite."

Moonie nodded eagerly. "Good choice! Can't go wrong with that. Classic."

As Monique turned to set the CDs aside, Moonie's eyes wandered, giving her a quick once-over. His lips parted slightly as if he was about to say something more, but then he caught sight of King in the backseat, staring right at him, eyes narrowed suspiciously. Moonie quickly flashed a grin and winked at King, but the boy didn't flinch, his frown deepening.

Monique, oblivious to the silent exchange, was busy collecting her things when Moonie suddenly chimed in again.

"Looks like the snow's really coming down," he said, casually glancing up at the storm. "Might wanna think about holing up for a bit. These roads are gonna be closed for a while, according to the news."

Monique froze, glancing back at him. "I don't know… my husband's on his way back. He should be home any minute."

Moonie smiled, too casually, pulling out his phone. "Not from what I'm seeing. Meteorologists are saying the roads are shut down in both directions. Nobody's coming in or going out tonight."

Monique frowned, her unease deepening. She looked at the swirling snow outside and then back at Moonie. She hated the idea of inviting him in, but the reality of being stranded in a snowstorm didn't sit well with her either.

King, sensing his mom's hesitation, shot her a pleading look. "Mom, we don't need him here. We'll be fine."

But before Monique could respond, Moonie smiled, leaning on the truck door. "It's no big deal, really. I'm just offering some company until things clear up. I wouldn't want you and King to be stuck here all alone. The roads aren't going anywhere for a while."

Monique sighed, glancing at the thickening snow outside. She didn't like the situation, but realistically, she didn't want to risk him driving in these conditions either. "Alright," she said reluctantly, "but just for a little while, until the roads clear."

Moonie's grin widened, like he'd won some kind of prize. "You got it, no problem. Just here to help."

They gathered the grocery bags, and Moonie made a big show of carrying most of them to the front porch. "See? Told you I'd take care of you," he said, giving her a wink as he set the bags down.

Monique forced a smile. "Thanks, Coach. I can handle the rest from here."

But Moonie wasn't done. "You know, Monique, you really shouldn't have to do all this alone. A woman like you deserves someone who's around, someone who can really be there for you."

Monique's smile tightened as she unlocked the door. "Yeah... I guess."

King stepped forward, standing between his mom and Moonie like a barrier, his glare hardening. "We're fine, Coach," he said, his voice sharp.

Moonie raised his hands in surrender, chuckling like it was all in good fun. "Alright, alright, champ. Just looking out for your mom, that's all."

They entered the house, and as Monique began putting the groceries away, Moonie lingered near the door, hands in his pockets. "You know," he began casually, "since the roads are shut down, I could stick around for dinner. Wouldn't want to impose, but if you're making something..."

Monique hesitated, glancing at King, who looked ready to explode. "I... well, I wasn't really planning anything fancy."

Moonie waved his hand dismissively. "Doesn't need to be fancy. I'm easy to please. Whatever you've got, I'm sure it'll be great." His eyes roamed the kitchen as if he were already making himself at home.

Monique bit her lip. The last thing she wanted was for Moonie to overstay his welcome, but with the snow piling up outside, what choice did she really have?

"Alright," she said finally. "But just dinner, then you can head out when the roads clear."

Moonie clapped his hands together, beaming. "Sounds like a plan! I'll help out where I can."

King crossed his arms, his frustration simmering. "We don't need help," he muttered under his breath.

But Moonie either didn't hear him or chose to ignore it. He pulled up a chair at the kitchen table, flashing a grin at Monique. "So, what's for dinner?"

Monique exhaled slowly, trying to keep things civil. "I was just going to make something quick—spaghetti or soup."

Moonie leaned back in the chair, as casual as could be. "Spaghetti sounds great. I love a good home-cooked meal."

As Monique started preparing the food, King shot her another look, his frustration barely concealed. "Mom, we don't need him here."

She sighed, her hands working quickly to chop vegetables. "I know, King. But the roads are closed, and I don't want him driving in this."

King frowned, glancing at Moonie, who was now flipping through his phone as if he hadn't just forced himself into their evening. "Yeah, well, I still don't trust him."

Monique paused for a moment, glancing at her son. She wasn't entirely comfortable with the situation either, but the snowstorm had left her little choice. "It's just for tonight, King. We'll get through it."

King didn't look convinced, but he stayed quiet, watching Moonie out of the corner of his eye.

Meanwhile, across town, Demetri and Cam were swerving through the icy streets like fugitives, snow pelting the windshield with a fury that made visibility nearly zero. The heater was cranked up, but the tension between them was so thick it could have iced the road over again.

"Man, I don't know about this," Demetri muttered, gripping the steering wheel like it might fly out of his hands.

"Relax, D. I got you," Cam said, rubbing his hands together like he was gearing up for a heist—which, knowing Cam, wasn't far off. He nodded toward the alley ahead. "There's the spot."

The alley behind Fletcher's was just as sketchy as Demetri remembered: dimly lit, damp, and reeking of beer and bad decisions. Cam spotted Gumbo, a dude who looked like he lived in a dumpster but had the latest iPhone pressed to his ear. He was leaning against a small U-Haul truck, waving his free hand around like he was giving stock tips.

"Nah, girl, I'm tellin' you, I'm premium-grade... Hello? Hello?" Gumbo shoved his phone into his pocket when he saw them pulling up. "Yo, what up!" he called out, grinning like a used car salesman. "I got watches, MacBooks, check stubs, addresses, bulletproof vests. You got bad kids? I got the switches—fresh from the tree! ADHD? Cured. Learning disabilities? Gone."

Demetri shot Cam a wary glance, still sitting in the car, half-expecting Lil Tone to pop out of the shadows with a baseball bat. "Where's Tone?"

Cam hopped out of the car like everything was cool. "Yo, Gumbo, you still got that stuff?"

Gumbo narrowed his eyes, his hand slipping inside his coat. "Why, what you heard?"

Cam waved him off. "Nah, I'm just tryna fill a wish list for the Make-A-Wish Foundation."

Gumbo's eyes went wide. "Oh, you then switched up? Gone good, huh?"

Cam grinned, flashing all his teeth. "Nah, man. I'm just better at being bad."

Gumbo cracked up, slapping his knee as he led Cam to the back of the U-Haul. But as they opened the truck, there he was—Lil Tone, muscles bulging, a nasty scar down his face, tossing boxes like it was his daily workout.

Gumbo pulled out a crumpled piece of paper and squinted at it. "Let's see. Limited-edition LeBron jersey... Xbox... Supreme shirts... Nike socks? Man, what happened to kids just wanting to be like Mike?"

Cam rolled his eyes. "That was a movie, fool."

Gumbo paused, looking at Cam's empty hands. "Wait... you ain't got nothing? Nothing?"

Cam's smile wavered. "You know I'm good for it. I'll hit a lick for you, just like when I stole those stereos, remember?"

Lil Tone froze, his back to them, and then spun around like a bull ready to charge. "I thought that was you!" In a flash, he lunged at Cam, shoving him hard against the wall of the U-Haul. "You've been ducking me for months!"

Cam's voice went up three octaves. "Watch my drip!"

Lil Tone leaned in close, his breath fogging the cold air. "You owe me, Cam. Where's my money?!"

Cam's hands shot up in surrender. "Twelve got it! I—"

Before Cam could finish, Lil Tone tossed him out of the truck like he was yesterday's trash. Demetri, watching from the car, saw Cam fly through the air and hit the snow with a thud.

Demetri's eyes widened, his hand hovering over the ignition. "The man's a magnet for trouble," he muttered.

Lil Tone stalked toward the car, his eyes locking with Demetri's like a predator sizing up its next meal. "Who's this clown?"

Cam scrambled to his feet, shaking off snow. "That's my partner! He was taking me to the money!"

Lil Tone squinted at Demetri, his jaw clenched. "Oh yeah? Picture man, huh? I know where your office is. Wouldn't want it to... catch fire, would you?"

Demetri felt his stomach flip. "This is bad," he whispered to himself.

Cam jumped in, trying to save the situation. "Relax, Tone! We'll get your money. Just give us some time."

Lil Tone didn't seem convinced. He turned to Gumbo. "Get the watch."

Gumbo pulled an Apple Watch from his coat and slapped it onto Cam's wrist like he was strapping on a hand grenade. "You got until Christmas. Midnight."

Lil Tone's smirk twisted. "Get me my money, and you'll get your little Christmas wish list."

He shoved Cam again, sending him tumbling back into the snow. Cam scrambled to his feet, bolted to the car, and practically dove into the passenger seat.

Demetri shot him a look. "What'd he say?"

Cam, breathless, waved it off like it was nothing. "Don't worry about it. We just need to make a quick pick-up. You'll get everything King wants for Christmas."

Demetri wasn't buying it. "What kind of pick-up?"

Cam hesitated, his grin faltering for the first time. "Okay, so... remember last year? The whole... bank thing?"

Demetri's stomach dropped. "You mean the *bank robbery*?"

"It wasn't a robbery!" Cam protested. "It was a misunderstanding. I didn't even know Tone was gonna—anyway, that's not important. What's important is I stashed the cash. But now we gotta get it before Tone does."

Demetri narrowed his eyes. "Where's the cash?"

Cam hesitated. "In an Airbnb."

Demetri's jaw dropped. "You stashed stolen money in someone's Airbnb?"

"Well, technically, it was a construction site back then. Now it's a house. And... a family's renting it for Christmas."

Demetri ran a hand over his face. "This just keeps getting better."

He glanced back at Lil Tone, still pacing near the U-Haul like a shark circling prey. Demetri was in too deep now. He had two choices: help Cam, get the money, and hope it solved his financial disaster—or walk away and deal with whatever turmoil came next.

Either way, Christmas was about to get real complicated.

Chapter 4: Heated Arguments and Dangerous Missions

As the snowstorm raged outside, back at Demetri's office, a mess of a different kind was brewing.

A tall, broad-shouldered man in a bulletproof vest stormed through the dimly lit hallway, his footsteps echoing off the linoleum floor like a harbinger of trouble. He looked every bit the part of a bounty hunter—bulky, serious, and with an air of "no nonsense." His eyes were locked on the door labeled "318 Kreative Studios Photography." The door was slightly ajar, just enough for him to shove it open with one forceful push.

Inside, a janitor, blissfully unaware of the impending danger, had his feet propped up on Demetri's desk, earbuds jammed into his ears, nodding along to the beat. A mop bucket sat idly by his side, completely ignored as the janitor stared dreamily out the window at the swirling snowflakes. His chair squeaked as he leaned back, eyes half-shut, pretending he was the boss.

"Call me the black Kodak!" he murmured to himself, chuckling at his private joke. "I damn near invented the picture! Tunnel vision, baby!" He was in his own world, oblivious to the giant shadow creeping up behind him.

Bunch, the muscle-bound bounty hunter, wasn't amused. He approached the janitor like a lion stalking its prey, his hulking frame casting a massive shadow over the unsuspecting man. The janitor, still grooving to his music, remained blissfully ignorant of the looming threat.

Without warning, Bunch leaned down and exhaled loudly right behind him.

The janitor's eyes flew open. In a split second, his chill afternoon morphed into a horror movie. He jolted upright, yanking the earbuds out as he came face-to-face with the human brick wall that was Bunch.

"Where's Demetri?" Bunch growled, his voice as deep and gravelly as an earthquake.

The janitor scrambled, trying to process this behemoth of a man towering over him. His feet were barely on the ground before Bunch grabbed him by the front of his uniform and lifted him effortlessly into the air like a rag doll.

The janitor's feet dangled helplessly, his mop clattering to the floor. "Whoa, whoa, whoa! I'm not Demetri! I'm just mopping! Demetri ain't here, man!" he squeaked, flailing his arms as if trying to swim his way to freedom.

Bunch narrowed his eyes, still holding the janitor aloft with one hand like a misbehaving cat. "Where is he?" he demanded.

The janitor, now sweating bullets, shook his head frantically. "I don't know! I swear! I just clean floors, man! He could be anywhere! In a snowbank for all I know!"

Bunch grunted and finally let the janitor down, who stumbled and almost fell but caught himself on the edge of the desk. He clutched his mop like it was a lifeline, his wide eyes never leaving Bunch.

As Bunch scanned the room, his gaze fell on a framed photo of Demetri on the wall, the one where Demetri looked like he was posing for a magazine cover—sharp suit, winning smile. Bunch's eyes narrowed further.

The janitor noticed where Bunch was looking and swallowed hard. "Uh… you wanna leave a message?" He offered weakly, gripping the mop tighter as if it could somehow fend off the giant bounty hunter.

Bunch didn't respond. Instead, he pulled a pair of handcuffs from his belt, the metal clinking ominously as he stepped toward the door. The janitor let out a relieved sigh as Bunch left, only for his relief to be shattered when Bunch suddenly spun back around, his face dead serious.

"You see Demetri?" Bunch rumbled. "You tell him Bunch is comin' for him."

The janitor gulped, nodding so fast his mop threatened to fly out of his hands. "Yeah… yeah… sure thing. I'll let him know!"

Bunch turned and marched back into the hallway, his heavy boots thudding down the corridor, leaving the janitor staring after him, still clutching the mop for dear life.

Once the door clicked shut, the janitor collapsed into the chair, exhaling deeply. "Man, this job don't pay me enough," he muttered, pulling his earbuds back in. He glanced at the snow falling outside and shook his head. "Tunnel vision, my ass…"

With that, he leaned back, propped his feet up again, and returned to pretending he was the boss—though this time, a lot less comfortable than before.

Back at Demetri's house Monique sat at the dining table, the tension in the air as thick as the snow falling outside. Coach Moonie had made himself all too comfortable, chatting away as though he'd been invited for the evening, though his presence had begun to weigh heavily on her. The road closures meant there was no getting rid of him anytime soon. Her mind wandered to Demetri—she couldn't help but wonder what he was doing, where he was, and more importantly, why he wasn't here.

As she stirred a pot of spaghetti, Moonie kept glancing at her from the kitchen island, offering more than just help with the dinner. "You know, Monique, you deserve more than this," Moonie said, his voice slick and warm. He was leaning against the counter, holding a bottle of soda, his eyes lingering on her as though trying to gauge her mood.

Monique barely glanced up. "More than what?"

"This." Moonie gestured vaguely with his hand. "Being stuck in a snowstorm, alone with all this responsibility, all these bags of groceries to carry... You deserve someone who's going to be here for you."

Monique gritted her teeth, keeping her focus on the simmering pot in front of her. "I'm fine, Moonie. Really."

Out of the corner of her eye, she could see King, seated at the table, shooting Moonie his best "get lost" look. She stifled a small laugh but quickly covered it up with a cough. She had no time for Moonie's attempts to flirt. The frustration of Demetri's absence was already pushing her to the edge, and the last thing she needed was to entertain Moonie's "help."

"Come on, Monique. We're both grown adults here. You don't need to do this alone. I'm just saying I could help you out," Moonie continued, moving closer to her, inch by inch.

Before Monique could respond, her phone rang, lighting up with Demetri's name on the screen. Her heart leapt, half with frustration and half with relief. She wiped her hands on a kitchen towel, picking up the phone with a sigh.

"Hello?" Her tone was sharp, but controlled.

"Monique, it's me," Demetri's voice came through, a little too calm for her liking. "I wanted to talk about something."

Monique rolled her eyes, knowing exactly where this was heading. "Let me guess. You're not coming home."

"No, it's not that," Demetri said quickly. "I just wanted to tell you I got a job offer. Six figures. It's for a shoot on Christmas Day. It could really help us."

Monique's grip tightened around the phone. She could hear the words but barely processed them. "You mean the same Christmas Day you promised King you'd be there? The same Christmas Day you told me—after three years—you weren't going to miss this time?" Her voice was rising.

"I know, I know," Demetri sighed, clearly torn. "But it's a big opportunity, Monique. You don't understand the pressure I'm under. This could fix everything."

"No, Demetri. What would fix everything is if you'd actually show up for once," she snapped, her frustration finally boiling over. She turned her back to Moonie, trying to keep her voice from shaking, but the truth was, she felt so incredibly tired. "You keep chasing all these opportunities, but what about us? What about King?"

There was a pause on the other end, and Demetri sighed again, clearly at a loss for words. "I'm doing this for you and for King. I don't want him to grow up wanting for anything, Monique."

"We don't need you to buy us things, Demetri. We need you to be here," Monique shot back. She glanced at King, who had gone silent, his face tense as he listened from the table. "But you're always somewhere else, aren't you?"

Before Demetri could respond, Moonie's voice interrupted from across the room, overly loud and far too friendly. "Hey Monique, you need help with that sauce? I can stir for you, babe."

Monique's eyes widened, and she shot a look at Moonie, her hand instinctively going to cover the receiver. "I got it," she said through gritted teeth.

"Who is that?" Demetri's voice sharpened on the other end. "Is that Moonie? What is he doing there?"

Monique felt her temper flare. "You're seriously going to ask me that? He's here because my car broke down and it's snowing like crazy, Demetri. He's been more helpful in one hour than you've been all year." The words came out sharper than she intended, but she didn't regret them. Not one bit.

"I don't want him in my house," Demetri growled. "I'm coming over."

"Oh, are you? You're going to come rushing home now that you know Moonie's here? Too bad the roads are closed," Monique shot back, her voice tight with sarcasm. "I can handle this."

King, who had been listening in silence, suddenly perked up. "Yeah, Dad. We're fine. Moonie's being... real helpful," he said, his voice laced with mock cheer.

Monique gave her son a warning look, but a small smile tugged at the corner of her lips. At least King had her back.

"Monique, just—" Demetri started, but Monique had had enough.

"You know what, Demetri? I don't have time for this right now. You figure out your job or whatever, and I'll handle Christmas." She hung up before he could say another word, letting the silence fill the kitchen.

Moonie, oblivious to the tension, sidled closer, leaning against the counter like he owned the place. "Everything alright?"

Monique forced a smile. "Fine. Just... fine." She turned back to the stove, stirring the spaghetti with more force than necessary.

Meanwhile, King was still sitting at the table, his eyes locked on Moonie, clearly not convinced. The young boy's mind was already racing, trying to think of ways to keep Moonie from getting too comfortable. Maybe if he broke something, or better yet, burned something—just a little accident that might make Moonie rethink staying any longer.

The snow had turned into a full-blown blizzard outside, but inside Monique's kitchen, things were heating up in more ways than one.

Coach Moonie, decked out in a ludicrous holiday apron that read "Kiss the Cook" with mistletoe stitched onto the front, was busy bustling around the kitchen. He had taken over the cookie-baking duties with a level of enthusiasm that bordered on ridiculous. Every few seconds, he shot a grin at Monique, who was oblivious to his cheesy attempts to woo her.

Meanwhile, King sat at the kitchen table, watching it all unfold with narrowed eyes. He knew exactly what Moonie was up to, and he wasn't about to let him get away with it.

"Monique, my dear," Moonie said, emphasizing the "my dear" in a way that made King want to throw something. "These cookies are going to be the highlight of your Christmas. Just wait until you taste my famous secret ingredient!"

Monique, totally distracted with setting the table for dinner, smiled absentmindedly. "That's great, Coach. Just make sure they don't burn."

"Burn?" Moonie puffed out his chest. "With me at the helm, these cookies are going to be golden perfection." He winked—yes, actually winked—at Monique.

King made a face so hard it could've cracked the windows. He wasn't about to let Moonie get away with his terrible flirting. He had a plan.

Moonie was at the counter, humming a Christmas tune to himself as he carefully measured out flour. King crept closer, his mischievous grin widening. He grabbed a can of baking soda from the pantry and swapped it with the flour when Moonie wasn't looking.

"Watch this," King muttered to himself, imagining the flour explosion that would send Moonie's romantic plans flying out the window. He darted back to his chair, trying to look innocent.

Unaware of the sabotage, Moonie dumped a heaping scoop of what he thought was flour into the mixing bowl. "Now, Monique, you just relax. Let ol' Coach take care of everything." He flexed his arms unnecessarily as he mixed the dough, giving Monique another "charming" smile.

Monique glanced over at him, half-listening, still focused on dinner prep. "Thanks, Moonie. Just don't forget the sugar."

"Oh, sugar?" Moonie shot her a smirk. "I could never forget the sugar, sweetheart."

King gagged audibly from the table. "Gross."

Moonie shot him a quick, almost annoyed look but kept his composure. "Just wait until you try these cookies, King," Moonie said, trying to sound good-natured. "You'll be asking for the recipe."

King rolled his eyes. "Yeah, right." He was too busy imagining Moonie's horrified reaction when the baking soda kicked in.

Moonie, in his obliviousness, grabbed the cookie cutter and got to work, shaping the dough into holiday-themed cutouts—snowmen, Christmas trees, and reindeer. He placed the trays in the oven with exaggerated care, as if he was performing some sacred culinary ritual.

King sat back, waiting for the disaster to unfold. But something wasn't right.

The timer dinged, and Moonie opened the oven door with a flourish, ready to present his masterpiece. King leaned forward, eyes gleaming with anticipation... but instead of a flour explosion, there was a strange, acrid smell.

"What the—" Moonie pulled the tray out, his face scrunching up in confusion. The cookies had puffed up into weird, lumpy blobs, their edges burnt to a crisp while the centers remained gooey.

Monique glanced over, finally noticing the strange shapes on the tray. "Uh… Moonie, what happened to the cookies?"

Moonie stared at them in disbelief. "I… I don't know! They should be perfect!" He poked one with a spatula, and it deflated like a sad balloon. "Something's not right!"

King tried to stifle his laughter, but it was already bubbling out. "They look… delicious, Coach," he said, his voice dripping with fake sweetness.

Moonie shot him a suspicious look. "You didn't have anything to do with this, did you?"

King put on his best innocent face. "Me? Nah, I'm just a kid. What could I possibly do?"

But as Moonie inspected the "cookies," he noticed something white and powdery on the counter. His eyes darted from the bowl to the pantry, where the baking soda can was slightly ajar. Slowly, it dawned on him.

"Baking soda?!" Moonie groaned, running a hand over his face. "King, you little—" He stopped himself, trying to stay calm. "You switched the flour with baking soda?"

King grinned from ear to ear. "Oops. Guess I mixed it up."

Moonie huffed, clearly annoyed but trying to keep his cool in front of Monique. "Alright, alright. You got me this time, kid. But I'll bounce back." He puffed out his chest again, though it was clear his confidence had taken a hit.

Monique finally caught on, chuckling as she surveyed the mess. "King, that wasn't very nice," she said, though there was a playful tone to her voice. She gave Moonie an apologetic smile. "Sorry about the cookies, Coach."

Moonie tried to shrug it off, but his pride was definitely bruised. "No worries, Monique. Just a little setback. I'll whip up a new batch in no time."

But as he turned back to the counter, King casually knocked over the mixing bowl with a little nudge of his elbow. Flour—or rather, baking soda—went flying everywhere, covering Moonie in a cloud of white dust.

Monique gasped, trying not to laugh. King, on the other hand, was doubled over in silent laughter, clutching his stomach as Moonie stood there, looking like a defeated snowman.

Moonie slowly wiped the powder from his face, giving King a death stare. "You're lucky it's Christmas, kid."

King just grinned. "Yeah, Merry Christmas, Coach."

Monique couldn't hold it in anymore and burst out laughing, shaking her head as she looked at the mess. "Alright, alright, enough with the pranks," she said, still giggling. "I think it's safe to say cookie duty is officially over for tonight."

Moonie, still covered in baking soda, sighed in defeat but managed to smile through it all. "Yeah... maybe that's for the best." He glanced at King, who was still grinning mischievously. "Next time, though... I'm making brownies. And you're not getting anywhere near them."

King winked. "We'll see about that." Monique gave King a look and ordered him to go and take a shower while she find a Christmas movie they could watch until Demetri arrived.

Shreveport's Backstreets - Same Time

Across town, Demetri's frustration reached its boiling point. He hurled his phone into the passenger seat and gripped the steering wheel like it was his last lifeline. The snow blurred the world outside the windshield as Cam rambled on about their "surefire" way to make a quick score, but Demetri wasn't hearing any of it. His mind was fixated on Monique's cutting words that echoed in his head like a broken record.

"Moonie's been more helpful than you."

It stung deep. The thought of that smooth-talking coach cozying up to his family while Demetri was out here in the freezing cold, trying to salvage the mess that was his life, gnawed at him.

"You good?" Cam's voice sliced through the silence, eyeing him warily from the passenger seat. "You look like you're about to snap."

"I'm fine," Demetri ground out, clearly not fine. "Just... drive."

Cam chuckled nervously, his energy jittery. "Relax, man. Once we get this cash, everything's gonna be smooth. You'll get King whatever he wants for Christmas, and you'll be the hero again."

Demetri shot him a sidelong glance, skepticism etched across his face. "This better not be one of your screw-ups, Cam. We don't have time for that."

Cam grinned, a little too confident for Demetri's liking. "Trust me, cuz. In and out, like clockwork."

The snow continued to fall in thick sheets, smothering the city in silence as they veered off the main road and onto a narrow, unlit backstreet. Each flicker of the streetlights cast long shadows over the deserted road, and Demetri's nerves buzzed with unease. This part of town didn't exactly scream "safe," especially with Cam leading the charge.

Staring a the road ahead, Cam let out a deep sigh, the cold night air biting at his lungs. "You know, D," he said, staring up at the dark sky, "I used to think I'd outrun all this one day—like I'd just pull off one big score and disappear. But it don't work like that, does it?"

Demetri, giving him a curious glance. "What're you saying?"

"I'm saying maybe it's time to stop running," Cam admitted, the weight of the words surprising even him. "I don't know. Maybe it's time to face it. All this... it ain't gonna end unless I make it end."

They rolled to a stop in front of a nondescript house, one of the many Airbnbs scattered across Shreveport. The house was lit up, Christmas lights twinkling in the windows, reflecting off the freshly fallen snow. Demetri narrowed his eyes.

"That look vacant to you?" he asked, his voice tight with anxiety. "Somebody's here."

Cam ducked down in his seat, squinting at the house. "It was empty... I mean, a couple months ago. Maybe a year..."

Demetri pulled the car into the driveway, and they both stepped out into the frigid air, the crunch of snow beneath their boots the only sound.

"Probably just renters," Cam shrugged, unbothered. "We'll get in, grab the stash, and be out before they even know we're here."

Demetri spun on him, frustration bubbling over. "You didn't tell me people were staying here, Cam. That's kind of an important detail."

"I didn't think it mattered!" Cam shot back, defensive. "Look, do you want the money or not?"

Demetri grabbed his cousin by the arm, his patience wearing thin. "Why are we here, Cam? I want the truth."

Cam wriggled out of his grip, throwing his hands up in surrender. "Alright, alright. I ran into some trouble, okay? I did a bid for robbery."

Demetri's face contorted with disbelief, and he turned to head back to the car, but Cam darted in front of him, blocking his path.

"Wait! It was me and Lil Tone. We hit a construction site. But before I got caught, I stashed the money here."

Demetri shook his head in disbelief. "I can't believe this. You drag me out here, into God knows what, and for what?"

"There's $300,000 in that stash!" Cam said, desperation creeping into his voice. "I owe Tone two hundred, but the rest is ours to split. You can get King those gifts."

Demetri's jaw clenched, torn between the quick cash and the looming disaster. "I have a flight in the morning, Cam. King needed those gifts today!"

As the two argued under the porch light, the front door creaked open. Standing in the doorway was a tall man, round-bellied but imposing, dressed like Santa Claus, and beside him, a strikingly beautiful Latina woman holding a glass of wine.

"May I help you gentlemen?" Santa asked, his voice smooth but edged with suspicion.

Demetri and Cam froze, exchanging a quick glance. Demetri's eyes flicked to the Airbnb symbol on the door, and he puffed out his chest, trying to play it cool.

"We were about to ask the same," Demetri said, nodding toward the Airbnb symbol. "We're guests here."

Santa raised an eyebrow, his confusion evident. "I don't recall this being a joint rental."

Cam stepped forward, his voice a little too casual. "Man, we're just tired. Drove forty miles in this snow. We just need a place to crash."

Demetri shot him a silencing glare and cut in, trying to salvage the situation. "There must've been a mix-up in the system. It happens with these rentals."

Santa, still suspicious, looked them up and down. "Right... I'll contact the owner and sort this out."

Cam jumped in again, his voice tinged with panic. "No need! We only booked it for a night. No big deal."

Demetri stepped in front of Cam, talking over him. "It's Christmas Eve. Let's not bother them. It's probably just a glitch."

Santa—Chris, as his wife called him—checked them out one more time, his eyes landing on the camera hanging around Demetri's neck. "You're a photographer?"

Demetri nodded, catching onto the shift in tone. "Yeah, I'm a professional. I do local work, but I also travel for shoots."

Chris's face softened into a smile, the tension easing. "Well, I'm sure we can work something out..."

As Demetri stepped onto the porch, a loud creak echoed beneath his foot, making his stomach flip. Chris smirked, gesturing toward his wife. "But it's really up to the missus, of course."

Heather, her wine glass swirling in hand, gave Cam a slow, lingering look, her eyes glinting with mischief. "They can come in," she said, her voice low and sultry, her gaze lingering on Cam.

Chris clapped his hands, grinning. "Welcome to Santa's workshop!"

Demetri chuckled nervously, but it died in his throat when he realized Chris wasn't joking. The smile faded from his face as they stepped inside, the door creaking shut behind them, locking them in.

Chapter 5: Uncovering the Kringle Secret

The Kringle family's Airbnb was nothing short of a Christmas fever dream—the kind that made you question if the holidays had gone too far. Every inch of the house was dripping in decorations—glittering wreaths on every door, stockings hanging from every available surface, and strings of multicolored lights crisscrossing the ceiling like a web of festivity. It looked like Santa's workshop had exploded, and Chris Kringle, dressed head-to-toe in a red velvet Santa suit, stood proudly at the door, welcoming Demetri and Cam inside.

"Welcome to our humble holiday abode!" Chris bellowed, his voice echoing down the long hallway.

Demetri forced a smile, glancing at Cam, who gave him a quick, uneasy nod. This was not going to be as easy as they had hoped.

"Wow, this place is... really festive," Demetri said, doing his best to sound impressed, though the over-the-top decorations made his stomach churn. The smell of pine and sugar cookies was so thick in the air it felt like they were walking into a gingerbread house.

"Yeah, great vibes," Cam added, looking around nervously. He seemed more jittery than usual, probably realizing this wasn't the ideal place to snoop around unnoticed.

Chris beamed, his cheeks rosy like a department store Santa. "Oh, we take Christmas very seriously here. It's our favorite time of year! Isn't that right, darling?"

His wife, Heather, glided into the room with a tray of hot cocoa. She wore an apron that read "Mrs. Claus," but there was something in her eyes—something off. The smile plastered across her face didn't quite reach her gaze, and her movements were almost robotic as she set the tray down. "Care for some cocoa?" she asked, her voice sweet yet strangely hollow.

"Thanks," Demetri said, grabbing a mug just to avoid being rude. He needed to get into their good graces, at least long enough to scope out the house.

"So," Demetri began, clearing his throat, "we were thinking, since it's Christmas and all, how about we offer you a free family photo shoot? You know, as a thank you for letting us... visit your lovely home." He tried to sound casual, but his heart was racing. He had to get them on board with this distraction if they were going to have any chance of finding the money.

Chris's eyes lit up like Christmas lights. "A photo shoot? Oh, how wonderful! We haven't had a proper family photo in years, have we, darling?" He looked over at Heather, who nodded stiffly.

Heather nodded stiffly, her voice mechanical. "That sounds... lovely."

Demetri shot a quick glance at Cam, who had already begun pretending to set up his camera equipment with more focus than a professional photographer on their best day. In reality, he was scanning the room, his eyes darting over every surface, searching for any sign of where the cash might be hidden. It was like an elaborate game of holiday hide-and-seek—except the stakes were a lot higher than finding an extra present under the tree.

"Alright then," Demetri said, gesturing toward the towering Christmas tree in the corner. The tree was so heavily decorated it looked like it might topple over under the weight of the ornaments at any moment. "How about we start in front of the tree?"

Meanwhile, outside...

Bunch, the bounty hunter, sat in his rusted-out sedan a few houses down from Monique and Demetri's place, peering through binoculars like a detective in a bad holiday TV special. Snowflakes were piling on his windshield, blurring his view as he aggressively chomped on a bag of fries.

"If I was a photographer... where would I be?" he muttered through a mouthful of potato, flipping through a stack of photos he'd swiped from Demetri's office. The snow continued to fall, quieter now, but thick enough that it coated everything in a calm blanket of white. Bunch rolled down the window and stuck his head out, eyes squinting as he extended his tongue to catch a snowflake. His attempt to savor the Christmas moment was rudely interrupted when a passing car splashed dirty snow all over his face.

The fries tumbled from his lap, his vape slipped through his fingers, and he sputtered, spitting the slush from his mouth. "Merry freakin' Christmas," he growled.

Back inside Monique's house...

Moonie was in his element, swirling a glass of wine like a sommelier who didn't quite know what he was doing but was determined to look good doing it. He and Monique sat cozily by the fireplace, the crackling logs adding a soft glow to the room. Monique scrolled through the TV, searching for a Christmas movie, while King was upstairs, finally taking a shower after hours of teenage procrastination.

Moonie raised his glass and smirked. "You know, a little teasing makes everything sweeter." He winked, clearly feeling himself. Monique hesitated, her glass hovering near her lips.

"I don't think you want me drinking too much," she teased, her voice soft but pointed. "The truth tends to come out when I do."

Moonie leaned back, letting out a low chuckle. "Well, they say the truth will set you free." He grinned, his eyes reflecting the firelight as Monique blushed slightly and gazed into the flames.

"Demetri used to say stuff like that," Monique said, half-laughing, half-reminiscing. Moonie scooted a little closer, leaning into the moment.

"Am I like him? Or... better?" He flashed a playful grin.

Monique rolled her eyes, laughing. "No comment," she quipped, taking a sip from her glass to hide her smile.

Moonie threw his hands up in mock surrender. "Oh, I get it! Not my business. But let me tell you this—a woman like you deserves the *best* a man can give." His tone was smooth, but sincere.

Monique smiled but kept it playful. "Uh-huh... is that so?" she said, swirling her wine. Her eyes caught a glimpse of the nursing degree hanging on the wall—a small but important piece of her story.

Moonie followed her gaze and nodded. "You know, my first wife was a nurse... one for eight years."

Monique chuckled. "Which one?" she asked, her voice light but curious.

Moonie paused, his smile fading just a touch. "The one that... passed. Stage four cancer." He let out a slow breath, his voice softening. "She checked everyone else but herself... Sassy as hell, too. Some people, you know... are irreplaceable."

Monique's smile slipped as the air between them grew more intimate. She poured herself a little more wine, listening closely. "I'm so sorry, Moonie. That must have been really hard."

He nodded, eyes on the fire. "It was... My second marriage? It ended because I couldn't stop seeing my first wife. Not a ghost, mind you—she was alive then. I married her again in the hospital, right before..." His voice trailed off.

Monique looked into his eyes, her heart softening. She set her glass down, fully immersed in his story now.

"What I'm trying to say is, your first choice isn't always your last. Sometimes the wrong choice brings you to the right one," Moonie said, his voice gaining strength. His hand inched closer to hers, testing the waters.

Monique blinked, her smile faltering just a bit as she stood up, heading toward the kitchen. "You know," she said, her tone shifting, "that's a nice sentiment... but breaking your vows is still cheating, Moonie. Doesn't matter the reason." She grabbed the wine bottle and gulped down a bit more, her cheeks slightly flushed. "Like Demetri."

Moonie followed her, glancing at her phone on the counter. "Has he even called you yet?" he asked, his voice taking on a sharper edge. "Must be something *really* important for him to miss Christmas Eve dinner..."

The Photoshoot Begins...

As Chris, Heather, and the twins Jr and Taylor — two kids about four years old, a boy and a girl—gathered around the tree, Demetri tried to keep the situation light. He needed to drag this out long enough for Cam to get a good look around the house.

"Okay, everyone, big smiles! Look like you're enjoying Christmas!" Demetri said, lifting his camera.

Chris threw an arm around his wife, pulling her close with a grin so wide it looked like his face might split in half. "We *love* Christmas!" he boomed.

"Yeah, I can tell," Demetri muttered under his breath, clicking a few photos. The lights on the Christmas tree flickered erratically, giving the room a slightly haunted feel.

Heather leaned in close to Cam, batting her eyelashes. "You know, Cam, you should get in the photo with us," she cooed, giving him a playful nudge.

"Uh, no, I'm good. I'm just here to take the pictures," Cam replied, taking a step back, his voice slightly panicked.

"Oh, come on, don't be shy," Heather said, sidling up to him, her hand grazing his arm. "You've got that rugged photographer look. Very... manly."

Cam nearly tripped over a stack of presents as he sidestepped her advances. "Yeah, thanks. I'll, uh, stick to the camera, though."

Demetri snorted, trying to cover his laughter with a cough. "Alright, let's focus on the family. Everyone say 'Christmas!'"

"CHRISTMAS!" Chris shouted, so loudly it startled one Taylor, who jumped in surprise and knocked over an entire pile of presents.

The presents tumbled down, causing the Christmas tree to sway dangerously. One of the ornaments—a glittery reindeer—fell off and shattered on the floor.

"Oh no!" Taylor cried. "I broke Rudolph!"

Demetri quickly snapped a photo of the havoc, figuring this might actually make for a memorable Christmas card.

"Don't worry, darling," Chris said, his voice booming once again. "We'll glue him back together. Christmas isn't Christmas without Rudolph!" Taylor looked confused "but you said if we break anything..."

Heather clapped her hands, trying to get everyone back in order. "Alright, let's try again. And Cam, sweetie, why don't you come stand next to me this time?" She winked at him.

Cam, looking more panicked than ever, stammered, "Uh, no, no, I think I'll just—"

"Oh, come on!" Chris barked, completely missing the awkwardness. "It's Christmas! Everyone should be in the picture!"

Heather gave Cam a sultry smile as she tugged him closer. "You heard my husband. Come on, Cam."

Cam shot Demetri a desperate look, but Demetri was too busy snapping pictures, his shoulders shaking with silent laughter. "Say 'cheese!'" he called out.

Chris, Heather, and the twins smiled brightly as the flash went off, but Cam was frozen, caught between smiling politely and trying to figure out how to escape Heather's grip.

Just when it seemed like things couldn't get more awkward, one of the strings of lights on the tree suddenly sparked and flickered, plunging the living room into semi-darkness. Chris chuckled, clapping his hands together. "Now *that* is what I call Christmas magic!"

Demetri used the distraction to step back and check the shots he had taken. Most of them were... interesting. The Kringles looked stiff and unnatural, their smiles too wide, the twins too solemn for kids their age.

"Alright," Demetri said, trying to sound casual, "why don't we switch things up and take some pictures by the fireplace? You know, get a cozier vibe going."

"Excellent idea!" Chris boomed, immediately guiding everyone toward the fireplace.

Cam breathed a sigh of relief, using the momentary shuffle to pry himself away from Heather. She gave him one last playful shove, causing him to nearly knock over a ceramic Santa.

Demetri clicked more photos, his eyes scanning the room for anything out of place. So far, no sign of the hidden money. But the way Chris kept pushing for more photos and Heather kept flirting with Cam was giving Demetri a growing sense of unease.

Back at Monique's house...

Meanwhile, back at home, Monique's holiday disaster was only growing. Moonie, having declared himself the "Christmas Tree Expert," had somehow made things worse.

"Moonie, I don't think you're supposed to put that ornament there," King said, his voice laced with barely concealed laughter. He was sitting on the couch, watching as Moonie stood on a step stool, half tangled in Christmas lights, trying to hang an oversized ornament.

Moonie, grunting as he tried to reach higher, stretched just a bit too far. With a loud crash, the tree teetered and then fell, landing on the floor with a cascade of ornaments scattering everywhere.

Monique, standing in the doorway with her arms crossed, let out a long, exaggerated sigh. "Moonie, I told you we could handle this ourselves."

Moonie, undeterred, scrambled to his feet and tried to prop the tree back up. "Don't worry, Monique! It's just a minor setback. We'll have this tree looking perfect in no time!"

King, still snickering, watched as Moonie picked up the ugliest ornaments King had dug out of storage and placed them haphazardly on the tree.

"You sure about that, Coach? Because it's looking more like a Christmas disaster zone over here," King teased.

Moonie grinned as he took a step back to admire his work. The tree was still slightly crooked, but he seemed to think it had a certain charm. "It's got character, that's all!" he said, brushing some tinsel off his shirt.

Monique, shaking her head but smiling despite herself, leaned against the doorway. "Yeah, character... sure." Despite the mayhem, it was moments like these that reminded her of the importance of family, of being present.

But still, she couldn't shake the nagging worry about Demetri. He hadn't called, hadn't checked in, and something told her he was up to no good. She glanced at her phone, hoping for a message from him, but there was nothing.

King, sensing his mom's distraction, rolled his eyes. "Mom, come on. He's fine. Probably just stuck in traffic or something."

Monique forced a smile. "Yeah, you're probably right."

She turned back to the Christmas tree, watching as Moonie struggled to untangle himself from the lights—only to trip over the tree once again. As King burst into laughter, Monique couldn't help but join in. It was disorder, but at least it was their kind of pandemonium.

Back at the Kringles' Airbnb...

After the photo shoot had gone on long enough to exhaust even the most festive of spirits, Heather declared it was time for dinner. The dining room, predictably, was just as over-decorated as the rest of the house. The table was set with holiday dishes, and the smell of roast turkey filled the air.

At the table were the twins, sitting quietly with unnerving politeness, their wide eyes fixed on their plates.

"Please, join us for dinner!" Chris said, pulling out a chair for Demetri. "It's Christmas, after all!"

Demetri forced a smile and nodded toward Cam. "I think he needs a minute," he said, watching as Heather tried to maneuver Cam into a seat next to her.

Cam shot Demetri a panicked look. "Yeah, I'm good right here, thanks."

As they sat down, the twins stared at Demetri with wide, unblinking eyes. Something felt off about them. They were too quiet, too still, like little dolls placed at the table for decoration.

Heather piled food onto Cam's plate, her fingers grazing his arm every chance she got. "I made all of this myself," she purred. "You should try the stuffing. It's my secret recipe."

Cam looked like he was about to melt into his chair. "This looks... great," he mumbled, pushing the food around with his fork.

Demetri needed an excuse to get away. "Actually, Heather, I was wondering if I could use your bathroom. Long drive and all."

Heather blinked, momentarily distracted from her pursuit of Cam. "Oh, of course! It's just down the hall, first door on the left."

Demetri nodded and excused himself from the table. He made his way down the hallway, but instead of going into the bathroom, he slipped into a nearby room, his heart racing. This was his chance to snoop around.

The room he entered was small, filled with old furniture and more holiday decorations. But as he scanned the space, something caught his eye—a door at the back of the room, slightly ajar. He approached it cautiously, pushing it open to reveal a small, windowless space. And there, sitting in a wheelchair, was an elderly woman—Maw Maw. She wasn't bound, but her frail hands gripped the armrests tightly. She muttered under her breath, her words slurred and difficult to understand.

Demetri's heart stopped. He crouched down next to her. "Hey? Are you okay?"

Her eyes, though cloudy, locked onto his, and she muttered something unintelligible, her head shaking slightly. She seemed desperate to say something, but her speech was too garbled.

Before Demetri could do anything more, the door creaked open behind him.

"Ah, I see you've found my mother," Chris's voice rumbled from the doorway, thick with unsettling warmth.

Demetri froze, his heart hammering in his chest. He slowly turned to face Chris, who stood in the doorway, smiling warmly, but there was something sinister in his eyes.

"This is my dear Maw Maw," Chris said, stepping forward. "She doesn't talk much anymore, but she loves company, don't you, Mom?"

Maw Maw's muttering grew more frantic, but she couldn't seem to form any clear words. Demetri stood slowly, glancing between Maw Maw and Chris. Something was very wrong here.

"What's going on?" Demetri asked, his voice low and tense.

Chris smiled, but it didn't reach his eyes. "Oh, nothing to worry about it. We take good care of her, just like we do with all of our... family."

Before Demetri could respond, Heather's voice echoed down the hallway. "Demetri! Are you okay? You've been gone a while!"

Demetri glanced back at Maw Maw, who was frantically shaking her head, her eyes wide with fear. But Chris stepped into the room, blocking his view, his smile unwavering.

"Why don't you head back to dinner?" Chris said, his voice cool. "We wouldn't want Heather to get worried, now would we?"

Demetri swallowed hard, knowing he had no choice. He nodded slowly and backed out of the room, his mind racing. Something was very, very wrong in this house.

Back at the dinner table...

Heather had leaned in even closer to Cam, her hand now resting on his thigh as she giggled at something he said. Cam looked like he was about to crawl out of his own skin.

"So, Cam," Heather purred, "what do you do for fun when you're not... taking pictures?"

Cam cleared his throat, desperately trying to think of an answer that would steer the conversation away from wherever it was heading. Meanwhile, Demetri returned to the table, his face pale but composed.

As dinner continued, the strange energy around the table thickened like the overly rich gravy Heather had poured over everything. Demetri tried to focus, but his thoughts kept drifting back to Maw Maw in that small, dim room. She wasn't bound, but her wide eyes and frantic muttering told him everything he needed to know—she was trapped. The kids, the twins, continued to eat quietly, their movements almost mechanical, as if they were rehearsing some unspoken routine.

Cam was not faring any better. Heather had settled in beside him, her hand still resting dangerously close to his knee. Every time she giggled or leaned closer, Cam would shift awkwardly, trying to keep a respectful distance, though it was becoming increasingly clear that Heather was enjoying the attention she was forcing on him.

"So," Heather asked, cutting into her roast, "how long do you two plan on staying in town? I'm sure there's so much more to see around here than just our cozy little home."

Demetri forced a smile, trying to think of an answer that wouldn't raise any suspicion. "Oh, not too long," he replied "After the snowstorm stops, we will be out your hair and just make our complaint with Airbnb tomorrow", glancing briefly at Cam, who looked like he wanted to crawl under the table. "Just a few more days, I think is all we need for our shoot."

Chris beamed across the table, his wide, unsettling grin returning. "That's wonderful! Maybe we can help you boys with your plans. I'm sure we could show you some local... attractions. There's plenty to explore around here."

Demetri's gut twisted. He couldn't tell if Chris was being genuinely friendly or if there was a darker meaning behind his words. The way Chris had spoken about "family" earlier still lingered in his mind. Who were the twins, really? Why were they so eerily obedient? And more importantly, what was the real story behind Maw Maw?

Heather tapped Cam's knee playfully, drawing him back into her web of flirtation. "Oh, you boys should definitely stay for Christmas. We could have a special little celebration just for the four of us."

Cam swallowed hard, flashing an uncomfortable grin. "I think we might have other plans, actually."

Before Heather could respond, Demetri cut in, hoping to shift the conversation. "Hey, how about we do a couples photo shoot after dinner, and then we can be on our way?" His voice was overly enthusiastic, but he needed to buy more time. "I can set up my equipment and then the lighting will be perfect, and it'll give us a chance to really capture the holiday spirit in your home."

Chris's face lit up. "That sounds like a brilliant idea! I can't wait to see the magic you two will create."

Demetri smiled weakly, his stomach churning. He needed to figure out what was really going on in this house, and fast.

Heather gave a slight pout, clearly disappointed that her flirting hadn't gone as planned, but she quickly masked it with a sugary smile. "Oh yes, a photo shoot sounds just lovely."

Cam exhaled quietly in relief, but Demetri could still see the tension in his cousin's shoulders. They were running out of time, and Demetri had a sinking feeling that they weren't the only ones with something to hide.

Back at home...

Monique leaned back on the couch, taking a break from the Christmas anarchy that was unfolding in her living room. Moonie had finally managed to get the Christmas tree upright, though it still leaned slightly to the left, and the lights were an absolute mess. King sat on the floor, snickering as Moonie attempted to untangle himself from the last strand of lights.

"Coach, I don't think wrapping yourself in the lights is part of the decorating process," King teased, his eyes gleaming with mischief.

Moonie grinned, still wrapped up in the mess. "Hey, King, I'm just adding my own personal touch. You know, getting into the holiday spirit."

Monique shook her head, unable to hide her amusement. Despite the disaster that was their tree, Moonie's infectious energy was actually making her feel better. For the first time in a while, the house felt... festive. Even if it was because of Moonie's clumsy attempts at holiday cheer.

"You've got to admit," Monique said, leaning back and laughing, "this is definitely the most memorable Christmas tree we've ever had."

Moonie finally freed himself from the lights and threw his hands up in triumph. "See? I told you. Christmas isn't just about perfection. It's about making memories. And look, we've got one right here." He gestured toward the slightly crooked tree, adorned with the ugliest ornaments King could find.

Monique's smile softened as she watched King and Moonie banter back and forth. It was nice, she realized, to have this kind of joy in the house, even if just for a little while. Still, her thoughts kept drifting back to Demetri. He hadn't called or texted all evening, and the gnawing feeling in her gut wouldn't go away.

Monique glanced at her phone again, hoping for some word from him. Nothing. She sighed, trying to shake off the unease. He was probably just caught up in work. But deep down, she knew it was more than that.

Back at the Kringles'...

Dinner was winding down, and the twins had finished their plates, sitting quietly with their hands folded in their laps, as if they were waiting for permission to move. Every now and then, they'd glance at Chris and Heather, as if seeking approval for their every move.

"Is it time for dessert?" Heather asked, her voice lilting like a nursery rhyme.

Chris smiled warmly at his "children." "What do you say, kids? Should we treat our guests to some of that delicious pie your mother made?"

The twins nodded in perfect unison. "Yes, Father," they said in eerie harmony, their voices flat and emotionless.

Demetri's skin crawled. There was something so off about these kids—something that didn't sit right with him. He glanced at Cam, who was doing his best to avoid any further interaction with Heather, but Demetri could see the unease in his eyes too. This whole situation was spiraling, and they were running out of time to figure it out.

"I'll be right back," Demetri said, pushing his chair back from the table. "I just need to... use the bathroom again."

Chris raised an eyebrow but nodded. "Of course. Second door on the right, down the hall."

Demetri gave a tight-lipped smile and quickly made his way down the hallway, but instead of heading to the bathroom, he veered off toward the room where Maw Maw was being kept. His heart raced as he approached the door, praying that Chris and Heather wouldn't notice his absence.

He opened the door slowly, the creaking hinges groaning in protest. Maw Maw sat in her wheelchair, still muttering under her breath. Her eyes were wide with fear as she looked up at Demetri, but there was no relief in her expression. She was too scared, too confused to understand what was happening.

"Maw Maw," Demetri whispered, kneeling beside her. "What's going on here? Are you okay?"

She muttered something incoherent, her hands trembling in her lap. Demetri strained to hear her, leaning in closer.

"They're... not... his children," she finally whispered, her voice barely audible. "They... took them... took me..."

Demetri's blood turned to ice. He had suspected something was wrong, but hearing it confirmed sent a wave of dread crashing over him. He needed to get out of here. He needed to get Cam, and they needed to leave—now.

Before he could move, the door swung open with a loud bang.

Chris stood in the doorway, his smile gone, replaced with a cold, hard stare. "Demetri," he said, his voice low and dangerous. "I thought you were just going to the bathroom."

Demetri shot to his feet, his heart hammering in his chest. "I, uh, got a little turned around."

Chris stepped into the room, closing the door behind him with a soft click. "Funny. You don't seem like the type to get lost easily."

Demetri swallowed hard, his mind racing for an excuse. But before he could respond, Chris took another step forward, his eyes gleaming with a dangerous intensity.

"I don't think you understand what's happening here, Demetri," Chris said, his voice soft but filled with menace. "You and your cousin... you're not just guests here. You're part of something bigger now. Part of our family."

Demetri's blood ran cold. "What are you talking about?"

Chris smiled, but it was the kind of smile that made Demetri's skin crawl. "You'll see. Soon enough. But for now, why don't we head back to dinner? We wouldn't want to keep Heather and the kids waiting, would we?"

Demetri's heart pounded in his chest as Chris opened the door and gestured for him to leave. He had no choice. He had to play along, at least for now. He had to keep Chris calm, to avoid raising any more suspicion.

But as Demetri walked back toward the dinner table, his mind was spinning. He knew one thing for sure—whatever Chris and Heather were planning, it wasn't good. And he needed to figure out a way to escape before it was too late.

Chapter 6: The Fake Photo Shoot

The tension in the Kringles' overly decorated dining room was thick, heavier than the rich gravy on the turkey that lay untouched on Cam's plate. The photo shoot was supposed to have been a simple distraction, a way to snoop around and find the hidden cash. But now, as the dinner stretched on, Demetri and Cam both knew they were running out of time.

Chris Kringle cut into his turkey with an unsettling smile, eyes glinting as he glanced between his wife and their guests. "So, boys, when do we get to see some of those photos?" he asked, his tone too cheerful, too curious.

Demetri swallowed hard and forced a grin. "Actually, I was thinking we could take a few more tonight. The light in the dining room is, uh, perfect right now," he stammered. His heart was racing, but he knew he had to keep up the charade long enough for Cam to continue searching.

Heather leaned in toward Cam again, her hand lightly brushing his arm like she was trying to butter him up for a Christmas cookie. "Oh, Cam, you're *so* good with that camera," she cooed, batting her lashes with the kind of intensity that would make anyone sweat. "Why don't you snap a few more photos of me and Chris? You know… something a little more… *intimate*." Her eyes sparkled with a hunger that wasn't about cookies or Christmas cheer, and it made Cam look like he wanted to teleport out of the room.

"Uh, sure, yeah, no problem," Cam stammered, fumbling with his camera like he'd suddenly forgotten how to use it. He shot Demetri a look so desperate it was almost telepathic: *Help. Me. Now.*

Demetri, sensing the impending disaster, popped up from his chair so fast it almost tipped over. "Great idea! Let's, uh, move into the living room," he said, his voice way too enthusiastic. "I've got some… *awesome* ideas for poses by the tree! Real festive stuff!" He was grasping at straws, but he needed to give Cam some breathing room—and more importantly, time to scope the place out. "Chris, how about Heather takes Cam in the back to check out the bedroom's… feng shui for the more, uh… *intimate* shots?"

Heather's eyes lit up like the tackiest string of Christmas lights. "That's a *fabulous* idea!" she chirped, already grabbing Cam's arm. "Come on, Cam, you can help me find something *festive* to wear. Maybe some mistletoe!" She winked.

Cam's eyes nearly popped out of his head, and he gave Demetri a wide-eyed look that screamed, *Really, dude?*

Chris, meanwhile, slowly rose from his seat, his towering frame blocking out the light like a human Christmas tree. His smile was tight, like he was trying to keep his face from cracking. "Alright then," he said, his voice slow and measured. "Christmas only comes once a year, after all." His eyes darted between Demetri and Cam with an intensity that suggested he wasn't completely buying the act.

Before anyone could move, Demetri clapped his hands together. "But hey, before we do that, why don't we get a few shots of just the kids? Gotta capture that holiday spirit while the tree's still standing!" He laughed nervously, hoping the kids would at least buy them some time.

Chris, clearly not entirely convinced but going along with it, nodded and motioned for the twins. "Alright, let's get a few of the kiddos first."

Demetri carried his camera into the living room, where the Christmas tree sat in the corner, looking more like a holiday disaster than a festive decoration. It was covered in gaudy ornaments, the lights tangled up in what could only be described as Christmas frenzy. The whole thing teetered slightly, as if one wrong move would send it crashing to the ground, taking everyone's holiday cheer with it.

Chris ushered the twins—Jr and Taylor—over to the tree. He pulled Jr in close with a wide grin that looked like it had been borrowed from a department store mannequin. Taylor followed, her movements mechanical, like she was on autopilot. Both kids looked more like props than participants, their eyes flicking between Chris and the camera like they were waiting for cues.

Demetri lifted the camera, trying to stall as much as possible. "Alright, kids, big smiles! Say... *Candy Cane Riot!*" he shouted, hoping to lighten the mood.

Jr's grin stretched wider than it should, while Taylor's face remained eerily still, like she wasn't sure how to smile anymore. Demetri clicked the camera, capturing what looked more like a scene from a spooky Christmas movie than a family holiday card.

Behind him, Heather was still hovering close to Cam, who looked like he might implode at any moment. She flashed a sugary smile. "Oh, Cam, why don't you come over here and show me how to pose? I need a little... *guidance*."

Cam nearly tripped over his own feet, scrambling to reposition himself with his camera as a shield. "Uh, maybe we just stick to family shots for now. You know, capture that... wholesome holiday vibe."

Demetri tried not to laugh, keeping his focus on the kids, who were now standing like statues in front of the teetering tree. "Alright, how about you two give me your best 'Santa's coming' faces?" Demetri encouraged, hoping to get a reaction from them other than sheer awkwardness.

Jr's face twitched into something resembling excitement, while Taylor's remained frozen, like she'd been programmed to stand still and wait for further instructions.

Just then, there was a loud creak from the Christmas tree. Demetri's heart skipped a beat as the over-decorated monstrosity began to lean... and lean... until it finally toppled forward with a mighty crash, sending ornaments flying and scattering tinsel everywhere.

"Whoa, whoa, whoa!" Demetri yelped, dropping his camera and diving to the side as the tree came crashing down in a glittering, tangled heap. "Christmas down!"

Heather gasped dramatically, though her hand still lingered on Cam's arm. "Oh no! Our beautiful tree!" she exclaimed, though her tone was more for show than actual concern.

Chris crossed his arms, his eyes narrowing suspiciously. "Guess we'll have to clean that up later... after the photo shoot."

Demetri chuckled nervously, standing up and brushing tinsel off his sweater. "No worries! We can make it work. It'll add some... rustic charm to the photos."

Cam shot Demetri a look that clearly said, *Dude, help me!*

Heather, still undeterred, clung to Cam's side, smiling like a cat that had found a mouse to toy with. "Well, why don't you come with me, Cam? Let's see if we can salvage this... festive disaster by checking out the bedroom setup."

Cam looked like he was about to hyperventilate. "Uh, sure. Why not."

Meanwhile, outside in Bunch's car...

Bunch sat in his car, cursing under his breath, furiously wiping dirty snow off his face. "This job better come with a bonus or I'm about to send Santa my own wishlist—starting with a flamethrower for this damn weather." His breath fogged up the windshield as he fumbled with his binoculars, trying to get a clear view of Monique and Demetri's house. But of course, they fogged up, too.

He squinted through the misted glass, his nose pressed up against the binoculars like a toddler trying to see into a candy jar. Just then, a car slowly pulled up, making Bunch instinctively duck down, the binoculars jamming into his eye. "Ow! Dammit..." he hissed, rubbing his face.

The car came to a stop, and out stepped Lil Tone and Gumbo, looking like the discount version of a low-budget heist team. They slinked toward the house like they were auditioning for a role in a spy movie, clearly thinking they were slick. Lil Tone peeked into Monique's living room window, pressing his hands against the glass like he was at an aquarium. Gumbo just nodded along, looking as clueless as ever.

"These fools really think they're James Bond," Bunch muttered to himself, shaking his head as he watched their pathetic attempt at being stealthy.

After a few seconds, Lil Tone and Gumbo scrambled back to the car, their mission apparently accomplished—whatever it was. As they pulled up to the stop sign, right next to Bunch's car, he leaned back in his seat and pretended to mess with his phone, hoping they wouldn't notice him.

"Man, he ain't home, but now we know where his family is," Lil Tone said, tapping on his phone screen like he'd just discovered fire. "Pull up the tracker app and let's see where Demetri's hiding. We'll get him soon enough." Gumbo, nodding as always, fiddled with his phone in agreement.

Bunch's ears perked up. *Tracker app? These knuckleheads are really trying to be high-tech gangsters?* He had to hold back a laugh. But this was serious now—if these two idiots were tracking Demetri, that meant trouble, and fast.

As soon as Lil Tone and Gumbo's car rolled down the street, Bunch's engine roared to life—well, sputtered first, and *then* roared. "Come on, baby, don't fail me now," he muttered, smacking the dashboard. He waited just long enough for them to get a bit of distance before he pulled out, following at a safe distance.

"Here we go, Bunch. Time to see where these fools are headed," he whispered to himself, gripping the steering wheel like he was about to enter the

Fast and the Furious. "Just gotta follow the breadcrumbs... or, in their case, the trail of bad decisions."

As Lil Tone and Gumbo weaved through the snowy streets, Bunch kept a steady tail on them, making sure not to get too close. He cracked the window a bit, letting the cold air snap him awake. The smell of greasy fries from the fast food bag on his passenger seat filled the car, but Bunch ignored it. There were more important things to worry about right now—like making sure Demetri didn't get himself tangled up in something worse than holiday drama.

Gumbo's car made a sharp turn down an alleyway, and Bunch slowed down, his heart beating a little faster. This was it—wherever they were going, it had to lead him closer to Demetri.

Back inside Monique's house...

Monique, Moonie, and King stood in stunned silence as the now-tilted Christmas tree blinked with a mix of colored lights that could only be described as a visual representation of holiday confusion. The tree leaned dramatically to one side, looking like it was seconds away from giving up on life.

Moonie, ever the optimist, clapped his hands together. "Well! It's got character now! You can't beat a tree with *character!*"

King snorted from the couch, snapping a picture of the tree with his phone. "Yeah, Mom, it's definitely *something*."

Monique sighed, shaking her head with a smile. "Well, at least it's still standing... *mostly*."

The house was filled with the sounds of Christmas—laughter, madness, and a toppled tree—making it clear that even when things went wrong, it was the love and joy that made it all worthwhile.

Monique sat cross-legged on the couch, her phone clutched in her hand as King howled with laughter at Moonie's attempts to "rescue" the Christmas tree. Moonie, now tangled in a fresh mess of lights and garland, was trying to stand upright, but every time he moved, the whole tree threatened to topple again.

"I've got this under control!" Moonie grunted, twisting awkwardly in the lights as King doubled over with laughter, capturing the whole disaster on his phone for social media.

Monique rolled her eyes, more amused than annoyed, and checked her phone again. Just as she was about to give up hope of hearing from Demetri, her phone buzzed—*finally*.

"Look who finally remembered they have a phone," she muttered, swiping to answer.

She pressed the phone to her ear. "About time, Demetri. Are you alive, or did you get lost in Santa's Workshop?"

On the other end, Demetri's voice came through, slightly out of breath and hurried. "Monique, listen, I've been meaning to call you sooner—"

"Yeah, yeah," Monique interrupted, "but what I *really* want to know is: What's more important than Christmas Eve at home with your family?"

There was a shuffle on the other end, and Monique caught the faint sound of jingling bells and—was that a woman's voice?

"Who's that?" she demanded, her tone sharpening. "Are you at a party or something?"

Demetri cursed under his breath, covering the receiver. "It's... just Heather," he mumbled, sounding more like a man caught sneaking cookies before dinner.

"Heather?" Monique repeated, her eyebrows shooting up. "Who the hell is Heather?"

Before Demetri could explain, Heather's sugary-sweet voice floated through the line. "Demetri, darling, we should really get back to the photo shoot! You don't want to keep *me* waiting, do you?"

Monique's jaw dropped. "Darling?" she repeated, her voice rising in disbelief. "Did she just call you *darling*?"

"Monique, it's not what it sounds like—" Demetri started, but it was already too late.

"Oh no. No, no, no. Don't 'Monique' me." She paced the room now, fuming. "You ditch me on Christmas Eve to go play *Mr. Photographer* for some woman named Heather? Are you kidding me?"

Demetri winced, rubbing his temple. "It's not like that! I swear—"

"Save it, Demetri. I know exactly what this is." Monique cut him off with the efficiency of a seasoned grudge-holder. "You think you can just 'shoot' your way out of this, huh? Oh, I know how this works. Next thing I know, you'll be showing up with a Christmas card *featuring Heather in a Santa hat!*"

Demetri groaned, trying to juggle the phone and the turmoil unfolding around him. Heather was leaning against him, still giggling, while Chris lurked nearby with a suspicious glint in his eye.

"Monique, please, it's... complicated. I'll explain everything, but—"

"You know what? Don't bother." Monique's voice was dangerously sweet now. "Merry Christmas, Demetri. Hope you enjoy your *photo shoot*."

With that, the call ended with a sharp *click*.

Demetri stared at the phone in disbelief. "Well, that went well..."

Meanwhile, back at Monique's house, she threw the phone onto the couch and took a deep breath, trying to compose herself. Moonie, now free from the tangled lights, gave her a knowing grin as he picked up the wine bottle and poured her a fresh glass.

"So," he said with a sly smile, "how's Demetri doing? Still saving Christmas one photo shoot at a time?"

Monique shot him a glare, but the corners of her mouth twitched, betraying her amusement. "Don't push it, Moonie."

Back at the Kringles

Demetri kept snapping photos, directing the family with exaggerated enthusiasm. "Okay, Chris, put your arm around Heather, and kids, smile big for Santa!" he said, his voice wavering slightly. As he clicked away, his mind raced with thoughts of the money. Where could it be?

Cam moved around the room, angling his camera in different directions, but his real mission was clear. His eyes scanned the shelves, the cabinets, the corners of the room, searching for any sign of the hidden cash.

"Let's try a shot by the fireplace now," Demetri suggested, his nerves on edge. Chris and Heather obediently followed, but as they moved, Chris's gaze lingered on Cam for a little too long, his suspicion growing more palpable by the second.

"Why are you so interested in taking so many photos, Demetri?" Chris asked suddenly, his voice lower, colder than before. "We've already got plenty of shots, don't we?"

Demetri froze for a second, his mind scrambling for a response. "Just trying to make sure you get the best possible family memories," he said, forcing a grin. "You know, it's all about capturing the magic of Christmas."

Chris didn't reply right away. He simply stared at Demetri, his eyes narrowing slightly. "Uh-huh. Magic of Christmas," he echoed, though his tone carried an edge of skepticism that sent a chill down Demetri's spine.

Heather, ever oblivious or perhaps playing along with the charade, chirped, "I think it's wonderful, honey. We never get photos this nice." She turned to

Cam, batting her eyelashes. "Do you think you could get a few of just me and Chris by the tree? Something a little more personal?"

Cam gave Demetri another pleading look, but Demetri was already positioning them in front of the fireplace. "Sure, sure, but first, let's get this next shot right here. Chris, Heather, just stand a little closer, and—" Demetri was interrupted by the sudden sound of a door creaking open behind him.

Everyone froze.

The door at the end of the hallway slowly swung open, revealing the dimly lit room where Demetri had found Maw Maw. She sat in her wheelchair, her frail form barely visible in the shadows, but her wide, terrified eyes locked onto Demetri's. Her lips moved, muttering something incoherent under her breath, her voice slurred and weak.

Chris stiffened. "Excuse me for a moment," he said, his voice dripping with tension as he marched down the hall toward Maw Maw's room. The atmosphere in the living room shifted, the forced holiday cheer evaporating into cold dread.

Demetri glanced at Cam, who took the opportunity to discreetly slip toward the hallway, camera still in hand. As Chris bent down to speak with Maw Maw, Cam ducked into another room, his heart pounding in his chest. They were running out of time.

Meanwhile, at Monique's house...

Moonie stood triumphantly in the living room, holding up a tangled mess of Christmas lights like a prize. "Who's ready for some Christmas karaoke?" he boomed, his voice filled with way too much enthusiasm.

Monique sighed, rubbing her temples. "Moonie, do we really have to do this? Can't we just... I don't know, watch a movie or something?"

"No way!" Moonie said, already plugging in the karaoke machine. "The holidays are all about spreading cheer, and what better way to do that than by belting out some holiday classics?"

King, lounging on the couch with a smirk, grabbed his phone and started recording. "Oh, this is going to be good," he said, grinning mischievously. "I'm about to witness the most cringeworthy performance of the year."

Moonie, completely oblivious to the teasing, picked up the microphone with confidence. "Ladies and gentlemen, prepare yourselves for the best rendition of 'Jingle Bells' you've ever heard."

Monique, still reluctant, crossed her arms and slumped into the nearest chair. "Alright, fine," she muttered, "but just one song, Moonie. One."

King snorted. "Yeah, one song too many."

Moonie didn't seem to hear him as he pressed play, and the tinny sound of Christmas music blared through the room. Without missing a beat, he launched into a loud, off-key version of the song, his voice cracking on every high note. "Jingle beeeells, jingle beeeells, jingle all the waaaay!"

King could barely contain his laughter, his phone recording every terrible moment. "Coach, you're killing it!" he called out sarcastically, biting his lip to keep from bursting out.

Monique covered her mouth to keep from laughing, but it was impossible. Moonie was so over-the-top, so earnest, that it was both endearing and painfully awkward at the same time. She caught King's eye, and the two of them exchanged a look of pure amusement.

Moonie didn't seem to notice the audience's reaction. He was in his own world, throwing in some awkward dance moves to match his off-key singing. "Oh what fun it is to riiiiiide!"

King burst out laughing, nearly falling off the couch as he held up his phone, adding commentary between gasps of laughter. "This is... this is gold," he choked out. "Best Christmas gift ever."

Monique couldn't help but laugh along, shaking her head as Moonie continued to butcher the holiday classic. For a moment, all the stress, all the worry about Demetri disappeared, replaced by the chaotic joy of Moonie's earnest but horrendous performance.

Back at the Kringles' Airbnb...

Heather's voice cut through the tension again, her flirtatious tone trying to disarm the growing unease in the room. "Demetri, you've got such a good eye for photos. Maybe we could do a private session sometime?" she suggested, stepping a little too close for comfort.

Demetri stepped back quickly, laughing nervously. "Uh, let's stick to the family shots, okay?"

Chris reappeared from the hallway, his eyes dark and narrowed. "Why are you really here?" he asked, his tone low and dangerous. "This isn't just about photos anymore, is it?"

Cam stood awkwardly near the entryway as Chris's narrowed eyes locked onto Demetri. The warmth of Christmas was quickly dissolving into something... *un-merry*. Chris seemed more suspicious with every passing second, and the overwhelming smell of pine and cookies wasn't helping.

"You really expect me to believe you're just here for pictures, and that you book this home the same weekend as me?" Chris's voice dripped with doubt, his Santa-belly not quite shaking like a bowl full of jelly.

Demetri did his best to smile, even though his insides were twisting. "Uh, yeah, man. It's Christmas, right? Nothing says festive like a family photo shoot... right... We can call the owners if we need to?"

Cam, standing by, was ready to sprint at the drop of a candy cane. "We gotta go, D," he whispered, fidgeting with his camera bag like it held the answers to all of life's problems—or at least an exit strategy.

Before Chris could respond with his full Grinch energy, Heather reappeared, practically skipping into the room with two steaming mugs. "Eggnog time!" she sang in a high-pitched voice that made Demetri wince.

Demetri let out a breath. *Saved by the nog.*

Heather handed Chris a mug, her bright smile temporarily neutralizing his sour mood. "Drink up, honey! You can't scowl on Christmas!" She gave him a playful nudge, forcing his frown to lift just a little.

Chris grumbled but took a long sip of eggnog. "This isn't over," he muttered, shooting Demetri one last warning glance. "After dessert... we'll talk."

"Can't wait!" Demetri said, way too enthusiastically, causing Cam to choke back a laugh.

Heather, blissfully unaware of the tension, clapped her hands together. "Now, let's get some pie, shall we? I made a special Christmas custard pie, and it's just *to die for*!"

Cam gulped audibly at her choice of words, but he followed her toward the dining room like a man resigned to his fate. *Pie or no pie*, they needed to find that cash and get out of this Christmas nightmare before they became permanent holiday decorations.

Meanwhile, at Monique's house...

Moonie was *in his zone*. The karaoke machine whined and sputtered, the TV lyrics slightly behind the beat, but that didn't stop him from giving it his all. He had the mic in one hand and his confidence in the other. And right now? Confidence was winning.

"FROSTYYYY THE SNOOOOOWMAN!" he belted out, waving his arms like he was on stage at Radio City. His voice cracked so hard, King nearly dropped his phone from laughing too hard.

"Man, *please* tell me this thing is recording!" King snorted, zooming in on Moonie's exaggerated dance moves as he stumbled over a tangle of Christmas lights.

Monique, sitting on the edge of the couch, had her head in her hands, shaking with laughter. "Moonie, I'm begging you—save some Christmas spirit for the rest of us!"

Moonie grinned, not missing a beat. "Come on, Monique! It's Christmas! The season of cheer! If this doesn't bring holiday joy, I don't know what will!" He twirled around, nearly knocking over the slightly crooked tree, which had already suffered enough at his hands.

Monique glanced at the clock, hoping this impromptu karaoke session would end soon, but secretly, she was enjoying every ridiculous minute. It was chaotic, it was off-key, and it was pure Christmas disruption—*her* kind of havoc.

King, now narrating between gasps of laughter, panned his phone over to the tree. "Oh man, look at this... this poor thing didn't stand a chance. Coach Moonie's Christmas magic strikes again!"

Just as Moonie was gearing up for the high notes of "Jingle Bell Rock," there was a knock at the door. Monique raised an eyebrow and stood up, still giggling as she opened it.

On the doorstep stood Mr. Donovan, the elderly neighbor from across the street. He was bundled up in a bright red scarf, holding a box that looked suspiciously like extra Christmas decorations. "Evenin', Monique," he said, peeking over her shoulder. "I heard the... uh, singing. Figured you might need some backup."

Monique couldn't help but grin. "Mr. Donovan, you have *perfect timing*. Moonie's just getting started on his holiday concert tour."

Mr. Donovan chuckled, stepping inside and shaking the snow from his coat. "Well, I brought over some extra Christmas lights... looks like your tree could use a little pick-me-up."

Monique glanced back at the Christmas tree—leaning to one side, half-decorated, with tinsel everywhere but where it should be. "Yeah, that tree's been through a lot tonight."

Mr. Donovan handed her the box. "Well, let's give it some holiday TLC."

From behind her, Moonie's voice rose up again—this time in an attempt at "All I Want for Christmas is You." The notes came out all wrong, sounding more like a yowling cat than Mariah Carey.

King let out a loud whoop of laughter. "Coach, no one asked for *that* under the Christmas tree!"

Monique gave Mr. Donovan a sheepish grin. "You sure you still want to help?"

He chuckled. "Wouldn't miss it for the world."

Back at the Kringles' Airbnb...

Demetri knew time was running out, and the thick scent of pine and over-sweetened pie wasn't doing him any favors. He'd had about all the "Christmas cheer" he could handle. As Heather insisted on serving up gigantic slices of pie, Demetri and Cam exchanged a look. They needed to make their move—and fast.

"Hey, Heather," Demetri said, putting on his best fake smile, "mind if I just snap a few more pictures outside? You know, with the snow and all?"

Heather beamed. "Oh, of course! Snow always makes the best backdrop! Chris, why don't you go show them the snowman the kids made earlier?"

Chris gave a slow, unnerving nod. "I think that's a great idea." His smile didn't reach his eyes.

Demetri swallowed hard, feeling like he'd just walked into a Hallmark movie where the villain wasn't trying to steal Christmas, but something much more sinister—like maybe their freedom.

As they headed out into the backyard, Cam whispered, "Okay, we need a miracle. You got any ideas?"

Demetri glanced around, noting the shed in the corner of the yard. "Check the shed. I'll keep them distracted."

Cam gave him a wide-eyed look, mouthing, *Are you serious?* But there wasn't time for debate. He gave a quick nod and shuffled off toward the shed, his camera dangling awkwardly by his side.

Chris followed them out, his eyes darting between the two like a hawk watching for prey. "You boys sure do love taking pictures," he said, his voice as chilly as the snow around them.

The snowflakes drifted lazily from the dark sky as Heather adjusted her scarf, tilting her head toward the camera. Demetri crouched awkwardly by the yard's tiny, over-decorated Christmas tree, trying to angle the shot just right. Chris stood tall beside her, his hands tucked into the pockets of his too-tight Santa coat, looking more like a bouncer at the North Pole than a holiday dad.

"Smile big! Think festive!" Demetri forced out, hoping the shoot would stall them long enough for Cam to scour the shed. "You know, *merry and bright!*"

Heather leaned into Chris, flashing a playful grin. "How's this for merry?" she purred, nuzzling up against him.

Chris didn't budge, his eyes never leaving Demetri, suspicion thick in his gaze. "We've taken enough photos, don't you think?"

Demetri felt the sweat on his neck despite the cold. Just a few more minutes, Cam needed *time*. "One more shot by the shed!" Demetri said, as he gestured toward it. "Really capture that rustic vibe."

But just then, *CRASH!* A loud clatter followed by a muffled scream echoed from inside the house, shattering the snowy stillness.

Demetri and Heather whipped toward the sound, but Chris was faster. "What the hell was that?" he growled, already storming toward the back door.

Demetri's heart slammed against his ribs. *That can't be good.* "Uh, Heather, why don't you—"

But Heather was already on her way inside, her holiday cheer replaced by concern. "Oh no, the twins!" she gasped, clutching her mittens like they might somehow help.

Chris threw a dangerous look over his shoulder at Demetri. "Inside. Now."

Back at Monique's house...

Moonie's grand finale—a disastrously off-key rendition of "Rudolph the Red-Nosed Reindeer"—was cut short when he tripped over the box of extra

Christmas lights Mr. Donovan had brought in. He went sprawling across the floor, tangled up like a Christmas package gone wrong.

King let out a howl of laughter, nearly falling off the couch. "Coach, you've got all the grace of a flying reindeer!"

Monique gasped but couldn't stop laughing. "Moonie! Are you okay?"

From his tangle of lights and tinsel, Moonie's muffled voice rang out, "I meant to do that!"

King wiped tears from his eyes. "Sure you did, Coach. Sure you did."

As Mr. Donovan bent down to help untangle Moonie from his festive prison, the room was suddenly filled with a loud jingle. It wasn't coming from the karaoke machine—it was coming from outside.

Monique stood, her laughter fading into curiosity. "What is that?"

King looked out the window, his face lighting up in pure glee. "It's Santa! And he's... stuck on the roof!"

Monique rushed to the window, her jaw dropping as she saw a life-sized inflatable Santa teetering dangerously close to falling from their rooftop. Apparently, Mr. Donovan had left it inflated *way* too high, and now Santa was dangling by one foot, bobbing up and down with every gust of wind. Moonie, still half-tangled in lights, grinned. "Now *that's* a Christmas miracle!"

Chapter 7: Danger in the Kringle House

Inside the House

Chris barged through the back door with Demetri trailing close behind, just as Heather rushed toward the hallway. They skidded into the living room—and stopped dead in their tracks, eyes wide with disbelief.

The twins stood frozen in the middle of the room, looking like two kids caught red-handed at a cookie jar. Surrounding them, anarchy reigned.

A holiday snow globe—one of those oversized, glitter-packed ones—lay shattered on the rug, glitter and fake snow spilling across the floor in shimmering waves. But that wasn't the worst of it. The family's stuffed Santa, a life-sized jolly figure with a mechanical "Ho Ho Ho," had somehow gotten tangled in the vacuum cord. Now, the Santa was spinning in circles like a possessed merry-go-round, yelling, "HO! HO! HOOO! MERRY CHRISTMAS!" as it whirled across the living room.

Taylor clutched her brother's sleeve, her lower lip trembling. "We didn't mean to start the Santa..."

Junior looked equally panicked. "We just wanted to see what the snow globe looked like when it smashed."

"WHAT?!" Heather shrieked, clutching her face like the apocalypse had arrived.

At that moment, the runaway Santa smacked into the coffee table, knocking over a plate of cookies. They scattered like little sugary grenades, and the Santa spun faster, tangling itself deeper in the vacuum cord until it tipped over and flailed on the ground.

"HO! HO! HELP ME! HO!" it sputtered, limbs twitching as the spinning slowed.

Demetri clamped a hand over his mouth to stifle a laugh. Cam would *never* believe this.

Chris stood there, jaw clenched, staring at the spinning Santa as if it personally offended him. "How—how did this even happen?" he growled.

Taylor sniffled. "We just wanted Christmas to be... special."

Chris turned slowly toward Demetri, eyes narrowing like he was about to say, *This is your fault somehow, I know it.*

Heather dropped to her knees, scrambling to gather shards of the broken snow globe. "This is a disaster! The twins' favorite ornament! Ruined!" she wailed.

Demetri muttered under his breath, "Favorite ornament? I thought Rudolph was the favorite..."

Chris, ignoring Heather's meltdown and the twins' teary-eyed looks, stepped closer to Demetri. "You better hope this mess doesn't ruin the rest of the night," he said lowly, "or it's not just Santa that's going down."

Just as the mechanical Santa let out one last garbled "HO... HO... NOOOO..." and powered off in a defeated wheeze, Heather turned to Chris with a desperate smile. "It's okay! We'll fix it! We just need—"

Her sentence was interrupted by a loud *POP* as the snow globe's remaining liquid sprayed across the rug in a frosty arc, splattering Chris's boots with glittery slush.

Chris's eye twitched, and for a second, it looked like he was going to explode. But instead, he let out a low, dangerous chuckle.

"Let's keep things festive," Chris muttered, his forced smile chilling.

Demetri knew that smile. And it didn't mean Christmas carols were coming—it meant trouble.

Chris's cold gaze scanned the room—and that's when it clicked: *Cam wasn't there.* His eyes darkened, and Demetri could almost see the gears turning behind his rigid expression.

"Where's your cousin?" Chris asked, his voice low and dangerous, like a warning bell before a blizzard.

Demetri's stomach dropped. "He—uh—he was getting some extra equipment."

Chris's face twisted into a suspicious grin. "In the shed?"

Demetri swallowed. *Damn it, Cam.*

Chris grabbed Demetri's collar and yanked him closer. "He's not just 'getting equipment,' is he?" Chris hissed, venom in every word. "You think you're smart? Think you can fool me?"

"Whoa, whoa," Demetri stammered, raising his hands defensively. "Look, I don't know what you think this is, but—"

"Enough." Chris pulled a key from his pocket and stormed toward the front door, locking it with a loud click that echoed through the house like a death knell. "Nobody's leaving until we sort this out."

Heather stood there clutching a broken ornament, blinking slowly, still trying to understand why her perfect holiday shoot was unraveling into madness. "Chris? What's going on?"

"Stay with the kids," Chris barked, his patience thinning. "I'll handle this."

Meanwhile, in the Shed

Cam was elbows-deep in a tangled mess of plastic snowmen, deflated reindeer, and old storage bins when he heard the crash from inside. He winced, praying Demetri could keep everything together long enough for him to find the money and get out.

He shoved aside another pile of holiday decorations—when suddenly, his flashlight beam landed on something unusual: a small, locked box tucked beneath a stack of old blankets. "Jackpot," he whispered, yanking it free.

Cam fumbled with the lock, frustration building. "Come on, come on..."

His fingers worked fast, but before he could pry the box open, he heard the unmistakable sound of the back door creak open. *Footsteps approaching.*

"Uh-oh," he muttered, shoving the box under his jacket.

Just as he turned toward the exit, the shed door swung open—and Chris loomed in the doorway, gun in hand, his eyes glinting with cold menace.

"Well, look what I found," Chris sneered. "A rat sniffing around my shed."

Cam's heart sank. "Hey, uh, funny story—I was just—"

Chris raised a gun. "Move. Inside. Now."

Back Inside

Demetri's mind raced as Chris forced him and Cam back into the living room. The front door was locked, their window to escape growing smaller by the second.

Chris waved the gun casually, but his message was clear: *You try anything, you're done.*

Heather peeked in from the kitchen, holding a tray of burnt gingerbread men like a sad peace offering. "Is everything okay?" she asked with a nervous laugh.

"Just perfect, darling," Chris said, his tone flat. "These two were about to tell me what there really doing here."

Demetri tried to keep his voice steady. "We don't know anything about—"

"Save it." Chris cut him off, his grin turning sharper. "I know why you're here. You thought you could sneak in, take my family, and waltz out. Not happening."

Heather, still oblivious, hummed a Christmas tune as she handed one of the cookies to Cam. "Here, sweetie, have a treat."

Cam stared at the cookie like it was made of TNT, but he took it with a shaky hand.

Demetri's mind spun. They needed a way out—*fast*.

And then, just as things couldn't get worse, there was another knock at the front door.

Chris's head snapped toward the sound. "Who now?"

Meanwhile, Outside with Bunch

Bunch had trailed Lil Tone and Gumbo's car through the snowy streets, trying to maintain a safe distance without losing them. His old sedan struggled in the snow, tires skidding slightly as he followed the pair to the Kringles' Airbnb.

His phone buzzed, and Bunch answered without thinking. "Yeah?"

"Still no sign of your missing kids it's been two months and the cops are assuming the worst," a tired voice reported on the other end of the line. "We're expanding the search radius, but—"

"keep looking," Bunch cut him off, his eyes locked on the taillights ahead. "I'm working it helps clear my mind. I'll call you back."

He hung up just as the radio crackled with news of an escaped convict. The reporter rattled off a description that sounded disturbingly familiar—medium build, brown hair, possibly traveling with accomplices.

Bunch frowned. *Where have I seen someone like that recently?*

Then it hit him. "It was the guy in a picture with Demetri that he saw earlier in Demetri's office."

"Oh, you gotta be kidding me," Bunch muttered, gripping the steering wheel tighter. He pressed the gas just as Lil Tone and Gumbo knocked on the front door of the Kringle house.

Inside

Chris nudged Demetri toward the door with the barrel of his gun. "Open it. Slowly."

Demetri's hand shook as he turned the lock and cracked the door open—only to come face-to-face with Lil Tone and Gumbo.

"Surprise!" Lil Tone grinned, shoving past him into the house. "Looks like the gang's all here."

Chris's eyes narrowed. "Who the hell are you?" Holding a gun to Demetri's back.

"We're the backup," Lil Tone announced proudly like this was some kind of heist movie. "Now let's talk business."

Demetri groaned. "Oh, for the love of Christmas…"

Cam tried to slip away unnoticed, but Heather latched onto his arm again, smiling sweetly. "Going somewhere, sugar?"

Chris turned to Lil Tone, his expression darker than ever. "You've got exactly ten seconds to explain why I shouldn't put all of you out deep into the snow."

Before anyone could respond, a car screeched to a stop outside. Bunch stepped out, his eyes scanning the scene through the front window.

Inside, the madness was reaching a boiling point. Then a sudden drumroll on the door.

The knock on the door echoed through the house, freezing everyone in place. Chris turned toward the door, the gun in his hand twitching slightly. His scowl deepened as Demetri, Cam, Lil Tone, and Gumbo exchanged nervous glances.

"Who the hell is it now?" Chris growled, his grip tightening on the weapon.

Demetri, sensing things were spiraling out of control, tried to force a grin. "Probably just… uh… carolers?"

Demetri took a shaky breath and pulled the door open, revealing *Bunch*, looking like a man at the end of a very long and ridiculous day. His nose was red from the cold, and his coat was dusted with snow.

"Evening," Bunch grunted, flashing his badge with one hand while holding a soggy fast food bag in the other. "Mind if I come in? Got some questions."

Chris didn't lower the gun. "What's this about?"

Bunch gave a slow, knowing smile. "Oh, just following up on a little situation. I think some folks in here might know a thing or two about it."

Lil Tone immediately threw up his hands. "It's not us! We ain't done nothing wrong... yet." He grinned awkwardly, clearly hoping the badge would keep things civil.

Bunch's eyes flicked toward Cam. "Well, well, look who it is. You're a long way from where you're supposed to be, buddy."

Cam groaned inwardly. Of course, the cop was after him. Perfect.

Chris stepped closer, blocking the doorway. "Whatever's going on, it's got nothing to do with us."

Bunch tilted his head, pretending to consider. "Well, that depends. Last I checked, one of you matches the description of an escaped convict, and someone else owes the IRS and has a bounty on their head." His gaze settled firmly on Cam. "Ring any bells?"

Heather, who was still clinging to Cam's arm, gasped dramatically. "Cam, sugar, you didn't tell me you were a fugitive!"

Cam shot Demetri a helpless look. "This just keeps getting better," he muttered under his breath.

Demetri tried to laugh it off. "Okay, okay, let's all take a deep breath here. No need to ruin Christmas with... legal stuff."

Chris ignored him. He shifted the gun toward Bunch. "There is no way I'm getting taken in on Christmas eve."

Bunch gave a lazy shrug, clearly unfazed by the gun pointed at him. "I don't know what you done but I come to chat with Mr. Photographer here." He nodded toward Demetri. "We've got some loose ends to tie up."

Chris's grip on the gun tightened. "He's not going anywhere."

Monique's House: The Karaoke Disaster

Back at Monique's house, things were taking a turn for the ridiculous. Moonie was now in the middle of what could only be described as an interpretive dance version of *"Rockin' Around the Christmas Tree,"* his tangled lights trailing behind him like the world's worst Christmas scarf.

King, still recording every second on his phone, was laughing so hard he could barely breathe. "Coach Moonie, you're a *legend!* Keep it going!"

Moonie executed a clumsy twirl, narrowly missing the crooked Christmas tree as he belted out the chorus. "Rockin' arouuuuund—"

His foot caught in the string of lights, and with a spectacular crash, he tumbled straight into the tree, taking it down with him in a blaze of blinking lights and ornaments. The tree hit the ground with a final, sad crunch, sending plastic pine needles flying everywhere.

"Moonie!" Monique cried, half-laughing, half-horrified as she rushed over. "You okay?"

From beneath the toppled tree, Moonie gave a thumbs-up. "Nailed it."

King was in hysterics. "Best Christmas... ever!"

Mr. Donovan, the elderly neighbor, shook his head in amusement. "Well, at least it's memorable."

Monique sighed, pulling lights and ornaments off Moonie's head. "We need to get out of here before you destroy the whole house."

But before they could untangle Moonie from the mess, Monique's phone buzzed again. She checked the screen and groaned—it was Demetri. She considered ignoring it, but curiosity got the best of her.

"Alright, what now?" she muttered, swiping to answer.

"Monique, it's really not what it looks like," Demetri said in a rushed whisper.

Monique crossed her arms. "Oh, so you're *not* at an Airbnb with a woman named Heather?"

"I swear, it's complicated!" Demetri sounded genuinely desperate now.

"Yeah, you're *always* complicated." Monique was done playing nice. "You better hope I don't find out you're spending Christmas playing Santa for some other girl."

Before Demetri could respond, a loud crash echoed through the phone, followed by Heather's voice shrieking, "The twins broke the snow globe again!"

Monique rolled her eyes. "Merry Christmas, Demetri. Try not to break anything else."

She ended the call and tossed her phone onto the couch, turning back to Moonie and the disaster zone that used to be her living room. "Alright, boys," she said, hands on her hips. "Let's clean this mess up before it turns into an insurance claim."

Back at the Kringle House: Mayhem Unfolds

Inside the Kringle house, the turbulence was building faster than a Black Friday sale. Cam, Demetri, Lil Tone, Gumbo, and Bunch stood like hostages in a standoff, all under Chris's suspicious gaze.

Heather, oblivious to the tension, floated between them like the hostess of a twisted holiday party, still offering cookies like they were peace treaties. "Anyone for more gingerbread?" she chirped, holding out the charred little men.

Cam muttered, "This is how I die—eating a burnt cookie at gunpoint."

Chris ignored him. His grip on the gun was steady, his scowl deadly. "Nobody's going anywhere until I find out what you're all really doing here."

Lil Tone raised his hand, grinning awkwardly. "Uh, technically, we just got here, so... do we still count?"

Chris cut him a look so cold it could freeze eggnog solid.

Heather clapped her hands. "How about a group photo?" she said with unnerving cheerfulness.

Everyone groaned in unison.

Just as Chris opened his mouth—probably to kick-start an interrogation—the chimney let out a loud *whoosh!* followed by a cascade of jingling bells.

The whole room froze.

Out of the chimney tumbled *Santa Claus*—or at least someone who looked like Santa, if Santa had spent the last hour doing somersaults through a coal mine. Covered in soot, the man dusted himself off with the dignity of someone who had definitely taken a wrong turn.

"Ho ho—uh, whoops. Wrong house!" he exclaimed, blinking in the dim room.

Chris's face twisted in disbelief. "What the—?"

"Is this 711 Rainforest Drive?" the soot-covered Santa asked, completely serious.

"No," Chris growled, gun still raised. "That's two houses down."

The fake Santa sighed and muttered to himself, "Man, I swear if they dock my pay..."

Bunch, who had been holding in laughter, lost it. He doubled over, howling. "This might be the dumbest bust I've ever seen."

Heather was delighted. "It's a Christmas miracle!" she declared, clapping her hands.

The Santa gave everyone a cheery wave and shuffled toward the door. "Well, folks, sorry to intrude. Merry Christmas, and, uh... I gotta run."

Just as the Santa reached for the doorknob, Chris leveled his gun at him. "No. You're staying here too," Chris muttered darkly. "Nobody leaves."

Santa threw up his hands. "Yikes. Is this about the cookies?"

At that moment, the twins—Taylor and Junior—appeared from the hallway, their little faces lighting up like Christmas trees. "Daddy!" they shouted in unison, running toward Bunch and tackling him in a tight hug.

Bunch knelt down, his tough demeanor melting as he held his kids close. "How'd you two get here?" he asked, his voice thick with emotion.

Taylor pointed an accusatory finger at Chris. "He said if we didn't pretend to be his family for Christmas, we'd never see you again."

Chris sneered, gun still in hand, but before he could say anything, Bunch lunged at him like an angry reindeer. "You *kidnapping grinch*!" he roared, tackling Chris to the floor. The gun skidded across the room, coming to a stop under the couch.

That was all the encouragement Demetri needed. "Time to go, Cam!" he shouted, grabbing his cousin by the arm.

As they sprinted for the front door, Heather trailed behind, waving her cursed cookies like some sort of sugary peace offering. "Merry Christmas! Don't forget your gingerbread!" she called out sweetly, completely oblivious to the mayhem spiraling around her.

Demetri and Cam hit the wooden porch at full speed, the boards groaning under their weight. Just as Demetri reached the steps, there was a sharp crack—one of the wooden panels splintered beneath his foot. He stumbled, nearly tripping, but then froze. There, in a hidden compartment beneath the porch, sat a dusty duffel bag.

Cam skidded to a stop, eyes wide with excitement. "The money! I knew it!" He yanked the bag free, slinging it over his shoulder with a triumphant grin. "Come on, let's go!"

Demetri was already in the driver's seat, the engine roaring to life. "Hurry up!"

Cam bolted down the steps, the heavy bag swinging awkwardly as he jumped into the passenger seat just as the front door burst open behind them.

Lil Tone and Gumbo barreled out of the house like two madmen on ice, their arms flailing as they tried to chase down the car. "That's our payday!"

Lil Tone yelled, stumbling through the snow with all the grace of a drunken reindeer.

Demetri slammed on the gas, the tires skidding wildly on the snow-covered road. "They're gaining on us!" he shouted, glancing nervously in the rearview mirror.

"Step on it, man!" Cam clung to the duffel bag like it was a life raft, his eyes wide with panic.

From the mirror, they could see Lil Tone and Gumbo, arms pumping furiously as they slipped and slid in the snow like deranged Christmas elves on a mission. Behind them, the disruption at the Kringle house continued to unfold. Chris and Bunch were now locked in a full-on brawl on the front lawn, crashing into the half-broken Christmas decorations, while Heather stood on the porch, still offering cookies to anyone who would listen. "Eggnog, anyone?" she called out, her voice a cheery contrast to the madness.

The tires screeched as Demetri took a sharp corner, snow flying up in an arc behind them. "Hold on!" he yelled, swerving to avoid a giant inflatable reindeer in the neighbor's yard.

Lil Tone and Gumbo, still chasing with more determination than coordination, found themselves dodging the same lawn decorations, narrowly avoiding a collision with an inflatable snowman. One of them slipped on a plastic candy cane, hitting the ground with a loud thud.

"We'll catch you, suckers!" Lil Tone shouted, scrambling back to his feet as Gumbo tripped over the inflatable snowman, which deflated with a comical hiss.

Inside the car, Demetri and Cam burst out laughing. "This is insane!" Cam wheezed, clutching the bag tighter as they sped away, snow spraying in their wake. "I can't believe we made it out of there."

Demetri chuckled, the tension finally breaking. "Next year, we're spending Christmas somewhere tropical."

Just then, a loud *thud* echoed from behind them, causing them both to glance back. In the rearview mirror, they saw Lil Tone faceplant into the snow after tripping over another lawn ornament—a giant inflatable snowman that wobbled dramatically before toppling onto him with a puff of fake snow.

Demetri shook his head, grinning as he turned back to the road. "Merry Christmas, suckers."

As they roared off into the snowy night, leaving behind the wildest, weirdest Christmas the Kringles—or anyone else—had ever seen, the distant sounds of holiday chaos slowly faded into the background. The last thing they heard as they drove off was Heather's voice, faint but still cheerful, calling out into the cold: "Don't forget your gingerbread!"

Cam glanced at Demetri, a grin spreading across his face. "Well, if this doesn't top the list of craziest Christmases ever, I don't know what will."

Demetri laughed, shaking his head. "You're telling me. Tropical, next year. No question."

And with that, the two cousins disappeared into the snowy darkness, leaving behind a Christmas night that no one—especially the Kringles—would ever forget.

Chapter 8: The Great Escape

Demetri floored the gas, sending the tires spinning wildly as the car fishtailed across the snow-covered street. The duffel bag full of cash sat like a ticking time bomb on Cam's lap. Both of them shared a quick glance—relief mingled with disbelief.

"We really did it," Cam muttered, still gripping the bag.

Lil Tone and Gumbo the two misfits jumped into their car—a rusty, old Chevy with half the paint peeling—and started the engine with a sputter that sounded like it could quit at any moment. As Demetri's car slid out onto the snowy streets, Lil Tone and Gumbo floored it in pursuit, their tires skidding helplessly for traction.

Inside Demetri's car, Cam buckled his seatbelt holding the duffel bag secure on his lap. "Why does this always happen to us?" he groaned.

"Because of you!" Demetri shot back, swerving to avoid a mailbox. He checked the rearview mirror. Lil Tone and Gumbo's Chevy bounced along behind them, the car door rattling like it was about to fall off.

Cam twisted in his seat to get a better look at their pursuers. "They're catching up!"

Demetri leaned into the gas, the engine growling as they skated through a sharp left turn, narrowly missing an inflatable Santa that wobbled precariously on a front lawn. "Hold on!"

From behind, Lil Tone shouted out the window, "You ain't getting away! That's *our* Christmas bonus!"

Cam turned back toward Demetri, wide-eyed. "Do you even know where we're going?"

"Nope," Demetri admitted. "But we gotta lose these fools before—"

BANG!

The old Chevy bumped into the back of their car, sending them skidding.

"—before *that* happens!" Demetri yelled, spinning the wheel to regain control.

The chase was officially on.

Cam stared out the car window, his fingers drumming against the duffel bag in his lap. "You ever think... maybe I shouldn't be doing this kind of stuff no more?" he said quietly, almost to himself.

Demetri gave him a quick glance. "Since when did you grow a conscience?"

Cam shrugged, shifting in his seat like the thought made him uncomfortable. "I don't know, man. It's just... it gets old, you know? Running all the time, looking over your shoulder. Ain't exactly what I imagined life would be like. Feels like I'm always one step away from messing things up even worse."

Back at Monique's House: The Final Straw

Meanwhile, Monique stood in the kitchen, her patience hanging by the thinnest of threads. Moonie, oblivious as always, hummed a Christmas carol to himself as he stirred what remained of the inedible mashed potatoes.

"You know," he said, turning toward her with a hopeful grin, "I bet if we added more seasoning, we could salvage these."

Monique pinched the bridge of her nose. "Moonie, you've already put a pound of salt in those potatoes."

"Yeah," he admitted, tasting a spoonful. "They just need a little more butter."

Monique closed her eyes and took a deep breath. "Moonie, we've been over this. Dinner's ruined. And I need you to leave."

Moonie gave her a sheepish smile. "Well, funny thing—the snowstorm outside kind of trapped me here. No way I can leave now." He leaned in, eyes twinkling with misplaced confidence. "Guess you'll just have to put up with me a little longer."

Monique glared at him. "Or I could throw you into the snowbank myself."

King, sitting on the couch, grinned mischievously as he scrolled through his phone. "Yeah, Coach. Mom's *real* patient tonight."

Moonie chuckled, still trying to play it cool. "C'mon, Monique. You know you love my charm."

"I will love throwing you out this house, Moonie," Monique snapped, barely restraining herself.

Sensing his moment to stir the pot, King grinned and whispered loudly, "Hey, Coach, I bet if you sang her another Christmas carol, she'd *definitely* let you stay."

Monique shot King a death glare, but it was too late—Moonie took the bait.

Clearing his throat, Moonie grabbed the karaoke microphone from earlier. "Alright, alright! One more song! Just for you, Monique!"

Monique groaned as he launched into a pitchy, off-key version of *"Baby, It's Cold Outside."*

King snickered from the couch, secretly recording every cringe-worthy second. "This is comedy gold," he whispered to himself.

Back on the Streets: The Wild Chase

Demetri and Cam sped through the snow-covered streets, fishtailing around corners and plowing through piles of snow like a couple of kids on a joyride. Behind them, Lil Tone and Gumbo were hot on their heels, though their beat-up Chevy looked like it might fall apart at any moment.

"Left! Take a left!" Cam shouted, pointing to an alleyway.

Demetri cranked the wheel, sending the car sliding through the narrow alley. Snow sprayed up in waves as they narrowly missed a parked truck.

Behind them, Lil Tone and Gumbo tried to follow, but their car skidded wildly. "Hold on!" Lil Tone yelled as they careened into a stack of snow-covered garbage cans. *CRASH!*

Demetri glanced in the rearview mirror and let out a triumphant laugh. "We lost them!"

But just as he celebrated, the Chevy lurched back onto the street, garbage flying from the hood as Lil Tone floored it.

"Oh, come on!" Cam groaned.

Meanwhile, from across town, Chris and Heather were in their own getaway vehicle—a sleek SUV borrowed from the Airbnb—and gaining ground fast. "We're not letting them get away with that money," Chris growled as he weaved through traffic.

Heather, sipping a to-go cup of eggnog, grinned. "This is kind of fun, isn't it?"

Bunch Joins the Pursuit

Chris and Heather had escaped and followed after Lil Tone and Gumbo. Not far behind, Bunch tore down the snowy streets in his old sedan, muttering to himself as he adjusted his rearview mirror. "These fools think they can outrun me."

He glanced at his phone, checking the GPS tracker he'd planted on Demetri's car earlier.

As his kids sat safe with their grandma back at the Airbnb, Bunch now had one mission: catch up with this ragtag group and end this nonsense before someone got hurt—or arrested.

"This better be the last time I chase these idiots through the snow," Bunch grumbled, gripping the wheel tighter as he swerved around a snowplow.

The car skidded to a halt just outside the town's outdoor ice-skating rink, spraying a wall of snow across a family of skaters. Inside the car, Demetri yanked the keys from the ignition, eyes darting to Cam swung the duffel bag over his shoulders.

"We gotta lose them—now!" Demetri barked.

Cam flung open the door, and they both jumped out into the freezing night. "On the ice?" Cam asked, staring wide-eyed at the rink filled with families gliding gracefully across the smooth surface.

"You got a better idea?" Demetri snapped, already sprinting toward the entrance.

They slipped and slid through the gate, tumbling onto the rink like two bowling pins hitting the gutter. Behind them, Lil Tone and Gumbo burst from their junker Chevy, slipping and scrambling like toddlers in untied shoes.

"There they are!" Lil Tone yelled, wildly pointing toward the ice. "That's *our* bag!"

Demetri and Cam stumbled forward, flailing like cartoon characters on banana peels. Each step was more humiliating than the last as they struggled to stay upright. They twisted and turned, arms windmilling for balance as they zigzagged between laughing children and disapproving parents.

Meanwhile, Lil Tone and Gumbo lumbered onto the rink, both immediately losing their footing. Gumbo flopped flat on his back with a *THUD*, his legs kicking helplessly in the air like a stranded turtle.

"Gumbo, you idiot! Get up!" Lil Tone barked, trying to scramble forward, but instead careening headfirst into a holiday display. *CRASH!* Plastic snowmen toppled like dominoes, sending tinsel and candy canes flying across the rink.

Right on their heels, Chris and Heather screeched to a halt in their borrowed SUV. Heather hopped out, cradling a to-go cup of eggnog in one hand, her face beaming.

"This is so festive!" she squealed, adjusting her scarf like they were on a wholesome Christmas date instead of a criminal pursuit.

Chris grunted, eyes locked on Demetri and Cam sliding away. "I swear, I'll get them."

Just then, Bunch roared up in his ancient sedan, tires spinning as it skidded sideways into a snowbank. He threw the door open and stepped out, slamming it shut with enough force to make the entire car shudder.

"Alright, that's enough!" he barked, flashing his badge as if that would suddenly make everyone behave. Spoiler: it didn't.

Demetri and Cam slipped their way across the rink, but just as they gained some momentum, Cam's foot caught on a rogue candy cane, and he went flying like a ragdoll. The duffel bag burst from his grip, sliding across the ice at high speed.

"No, no, no!" Cam shouted, crawling after it on all fours.

Lil Tone spotted the bag and dove toward it, flinging himself through the air with reckless abandon. "Mine!" he cried.

He missed.

Instead, he slammed into a line of inflatable penguins, sending them toppling over in slow motion. *WHUMP, WHUMP, WHUMP.* Gumbo tripped over the last one, face-planting into the ice with a groan.

Chris spotted the bag, his eyes lighting up with greedy glee. "It's mine!" he growled, lunging forward just as Bunch tackled him from the side.

The two men went skidding across the rink, arms and legs tangled like a pair of uncoordinated figure skaters. They spun in circles before crashing into the boards with a *WHAM.*

"Stay down!" Bunch snarled, but Chris wasn't done.

In the heat of everything Heather had found and put on a pair of skates. Still sipping her eggnog, she skated gracefully toward them with the finesse of someone completely detached from reality. "You boys are going to catch a cold out here!" she chirped, twirling in place like a figure-skating champion.

Cam scrambled to his feet, grabbed the duffel bag, and sprinted toward the exit, skidding and sliding like a man on a mission. "We gotta go, now!" he shouted to Demetri.

Demetri grabbed Cam's arm, yanking him forward. "Move, before this gets any worse!"

From behind them, Lil Tone and Gumbo were already back in pursuit, slipping and tripping over every stray piece of tinsel and inflatable in their path. "That money's ours!" Lil Tone howled, dodging a toddler on a sled.

The crowd around them began to notice the commotion—children gasping, parents shouting, inflatable snowmen wobbling. It was a Christmas disaster in full swing.

"Get 'em!" Gumbo yelled as they gained speed, looking more like drunken reindeer than men on a mission.

Demetri and Cam skidded off the rink and bolted toward a small wooden bridge that overlooked the skating area. The snow crunched under their boots as they clambered up the incline, the duffel bag swinging wildly between them.

"We made it!" Cam gasped, panting for breath.

But just as they reached the car on the other side, Lil Tone and Gumbo appeared out of nowhere, tackling them to the ground. "Gotcha!" Lil Tone wheezed, pinning Demetri down.

Before anyone could catch their breath, Chris stormed up the bridge, gun in hand. "Hand over that bag," he growled, his eyes wild. "Now!"

Cam gripped the duffel tighter. "You don't wanna do this, man!"

Bunch appeared next, stepping out from the shadows. "Put the gun down" Chris turned the gun to Bunch. "You got your kids back. Walk away while you still can." Lil Tone interrupted.

"I worked too hard for that money!" Lil Tone shouted, his voice cracking.

Chris swung the gun toward Lil Tone, his face twisted in rage. "I don't think you're in any position to negotiate."

Demetri's eyes flicked to the skating rink below. Families were laughing, children throwing snowballs, couples skating hand-in-hand. For a brief second, he thought about King—about how much he missed Christmas with his family.

Then, without warning, Demetri made his move.

He yanked the duffel bag from Cam, unzipped it, and in one fluid motion, flung it high into the air.

"No!" Chris screamed, his eyes widening in disbelief.

The bag sailed over the edge of the bridge, and in a breathtakingly chaotic moment, hundreds of bills burst free. Twenties and hundreds fluttered through the air like confetti, raining down on the skaters below.

"Merry Christmas!" Demetri shouted with a grin as the crowd erupted into cheers.

Chris froze, staring helplessly at the falling cash. "No... no!"

Bunch didn't hesitate. He tackled Chris to the ground, slapping a pair of handcuffs on him. "You're done," Bunch growled.

Lil Tone and Gumbo, eyes wide with greed, sprinted down the bridge, shoving kids out of the way as they tried to grab as much money as they could.

Heather, still cradling her eggnog, skated gracefully into the chaos, offering gingerbread cookies to confused police officers. "Anyone for a snack?"

Just as Lil Tone and Gumbo stuffed wads of cash into their jackets, a voice rang out across the rink.

"FREEZE! Hands up!"

The two men turned slowly, realizing they were surrounded by half a dozen cops—who had gathered for an ice-skating event hosted by the police department.

Lil Tone dropped the money with a defeated sigh. "You've got to be kidding me."

Gumbo groaned. "We really should've stayed home."

Heather appeared and jumped on Bunch's back only to be tossed to the ground and put in cuffs. Bunch tightened the cuffs on Chris's wrists, his jaw clenched with barely restrained fury. He glanced at Demetri and Cam, who stood frozen with their hands raised, waiting for what came next. For a moment, Bunch considered hauling all of them in—every one of these fools had been neck-deep in this mess. But then his gaze drifted toward Chris, the man who had *kidnapped his children* and used them as pawns in this twisted Christmas scheme. The memory of Taylor's frightened voice—"He said we'd never see you again"—echoed in his mind, igniting a slow burn in his chest.

Bunch shot Demetri and Cam a hard look, his grip tightening around the gun in his hand. "You two idiots ain't worth the paperwork," he muttered under his breath. He pointed the gun toward the street. "Get lost before I change my mind."

Cam blinked, stunned. "Wait, seriously?"

"Do I *look* like I'm in the mood to explain this mess to the chief?" Bunch snapped, nodding toward Chris with pure disgust. "That's the real problem right there. Now go. Before I make it *your* problem too."

Demetri didn't wait for a second invitation. He grabbed Cam by the collar, dragging him toward the car. "Let's go, let's go!" Their laughter echoed into the snowy night as they bolted toward freedom, leaving Bunch standing over Chris with cuffs in one hand and rage boiling just beneath the surface.

Bunch leaned down to whisper in Chris's ear, his voice as cold as the snow beneath them. "You took my kids. That makes this personal."

Monique paced the living room, frustration simmering beneath the surface. King sat on the couch with a mischievous grin, scrolling through the video he had just recorded of Moonie's latest off-key karaoke disaster. Moonie leaned back smugly in an armchair, arms crossed as if he had all the time in the world, despite the chaos he had caused.

"You know, Monique," Moonie said with an arrogant smirk, "you really don't deserve a guy like Demetri. He's always out chasing nonsense. I bet you'd be better off with someone... more dependable." His eyes gleamed with smug confidence as he leaned in closer.

Monique's jaw clenched. "Moonie, I swear if you don't—"

At that moment, the front door flew open with a gust of cold wind—and there stood Demetri, his eyes blazing with determination, the night's insanity still clinging to his clothes.

Moonie smirked, rising slowly from the chair. "Look who finally decided to come home. Bet you were too busy playing hero to remember who's really been keeping Monique company, huh?" He stepped toward Demetri, puffing his chest out. "She deserves better. And honestly, you don't even know what you're missing."

Demetri's fists clenched at his sides, his knuckles whitening. "You've got about three seconds to step away from my family," he growled through gritted teeth, his voice low and deadly.

Moonie sneered, trying to make one last move toward Monique. "Oh, come on, man. Let's be honest. You think you're good enough for her? You don't even—"

WHAM!

Demetri's punch landed square on Moonie's jaw with a sickening *crack*, sending him crashing into the armchair. Moonie clutched his face, groaning as he scrambled to his feet, holding his jaw in disbelief.

"Get. Out," Demetri snarled, his voice like a warning bell before a storm. "Now."

Moonie staggered toward the door, muttering under his breath. "You'll regret this... I was just trying to help," he said weakly, rubbing his jaw.

"Yeah, well," King piped up from the couch, barely hiding his grin, "consider this your severance package, Coach. Don't let the snowbank hit you on the way out."

Moonie shot King a withering glare, but King just smirked and gave him a little wave.

Monique crossed her arms, watching as Moonie finally slinked out the door. The sound of it slamming shut behind him was like a weight lifted off her shoulders. She exhaled deeply, turning toward Demetri with a look that was half exasperation, half relief.

Demetri let out a breath he didn't realize he'd been holding. "I should've punched him a long time ago."

Monique arched a brow. "Yeah, you think?"

Demetri crossed the room slowly, his expression softening as he approached Monique. "Listen, Mo... I know I've been screwing things up. And I know money won't fix everything." He reached for her hand, holding it gently. "I'm done with the hustles, the shortcuts. I just want to be here. With you and King. Every Christmas. Every day."

With the storm behind them—both literally and figuratively—Demetri, Monique, and King headed out into the backyard. The snow glistened under the dim light from the house, a rare, peaceful silence falling over the neighborhood.

King threw a snowball playfully at his dad, grinning ear to ear. "I bet you can't hit me back!"

"Oh, I'll show you," Demetri teased, packing a snowball.

As they played, Demetri's phone buzzed in his pocket. He fished it out, seeing an unfamiliar number on the screen. "Hold up," he told King, raising a finger as he answered.

"Hello? Yeah, this is Demetri." His brow furrowed for a moment, and then a slow smile spread across his face. "Wait, really? You're offering me the position?"

Monique looked over, curious. "What's that?"

Demetri mouthed the words, *The job*. His excitement was evident, but he kept his cool on the phone. "Thank you. I accept. And don't worry, I'll be staying in town. No more traveling."

He ended the call and turned to Monique and King, his smile as wide as the snowy horizon. "I got a new job offer. And I'll be home. Every Christmas, for now on."

Monique's face softened, and King whooped, tackling Demetri in a playful hug. "About time, Dad!"

Monique joined the hug, wrapping her arms around both of them. "This is all I ever wanted."

Feeling lighter than they had in months, the three of them headed back inside the warm house. But as they stepped into the living room, they all froze in disbelief.

The Christmas tree—bare just hours earlier—was now surrounded by a mountain of presents, beautifully wrapped with shiny bows and festive paper. King's eyes widened in shock. "What the...?"

Monique looked at Demetri, confusion spreading across her face. "Where did all these come from?"

Demetri shook his head. "I have no idea."

King rushed to the tree and began tearing into the gifts. His excited shout echoed through the room as he pulled out a jersey—the exact one he had been asking for. "Mom! Dad! It's the jersey I wanted!"

Monique's jaw dropped as she knelt beside him, holding up another wrapped gift with her name on it. "This is... how? Where did all this come from?"

Demetri stood there, bewildered, scanning the room for any sign of an explanation. "I swear I didn't do this," he said, as much to himself as to Monique.

They exchanged looks, trying to make sense of the Christmas miracle they'd stumbled into.

Outside: A Quiet Goodbye

Unbeknownst to them, Cam was outside, sitting behind the wheel of Lil Tone's rusty U-Haul. The engine rumbled quietly, and inside the truck, the seats were bare—no gifts, no bags, just Cam, staring out at the snow-covered street ahead of him.

He exhaled deeply, watching his breath fog up the windshield. Turning his head, he gave the house one last glance—a small, satisfied smile playing at the corner of his lips.

He had done it. He had left the gifts—every single one—and given his family the Christmas they deserved. No explanations. No glory. Just love, in the only way he knew how to give it.

With a quiet resolve, Cam shifted the truck into gear. He had made his decision. There were things he had to set right—starting with himself.

As the U-Haul rumbled down the snowy street, Cam glanced at the rearview mirror, catching a final glimpse of the house. He imagined King tearing into the presents, Monique laughing, and Demetri standing there, confused but happy. For the first time in a long while, it felt good to do something right.

"Guess this is my Christmas gift," Cam whispered, to himself. He exhaled slowly, the fog from his breath swirling in the cold air. "Time to pay what I owe." With a nod to himself, he pressed the gas and headed toward the station—ready to turn himself in and, for the first time, stop running.

As the U-Haul slowly pulled away into the snowy night, Cam whispered under his breath, "Time to do the right thing." He had decided to turn himself in and finally face the music.

Bunch's New Beginning

Meanwhile, across town, Bunch sat with his kids, Taylor and Junior, both wrapped in thick blankets as they huddled around the fireplace at Maw Maw's. The chaos of the night was finally behind him, and for the first time in months, Bunch felt a sense of peace.

Junior looked up at him with wide eyes. "Are we really staying with you now, Daddy?"

Bunch smiled, ruffling his son's hair. "Yeah, buddy. For good this time."

Taylor snuggled closer, her little voice soft. "No more bad guys?"

"No more bad guys," Bunch promised, holding them both tight. "Just us. And maybe... some hot cocoa."

His heart felt lighter than it had in years. This was what mattered. His kids, safe and sound.

A New Beginning

Inside the house, Monique, Demetri, and King sat on the floor, surrounded by wrapping paper and joy. Laughter filled the air as they enjoyed their unexpected gifts, the weight of the past few months lifting with every smile and hug.

Demetri wrapped an arm around Monique, pulling her close. King leaned into them both, clutching his new jersey like it was the most valuable thing in the world.

For the first time in a long time, everything felt exactly as it should.

"Merry Christmas," Demetri whispered.

Monique smiled, resting her head on his shoulder. "Merry Christmas."

King looked up at them with a playful grin. "So... does this mean I'm off the hook for cleaning my room?"

Demetri chuckled. "Not a chance, kid."

As they sat there, basking in the warmth of their little family, the snow continued to fall gently outside—covering the streets, the rooftops, and the tire tracks of a U-Haul disappearing into the night.

And somewhere out there, Cam was making his way toward redemption, leaving behind more than just presents—he had left behind hope, love, and the promise of better days ahead.

The End

Also by Ike Ojukwu

Shattered Dome
June to April: Bound by Obsession
The Demon's Whisper: Bound by Shadows
Demetri's Picture Perfect Christmas

Watch for more at www.k1films.com.

About the Author

Ikemefuna Ojukwu Jr (Pen Name: Ike Ojukwu)

Born in Lafayette, Louisiana, and raised in Jennings, Louisiana, Ike Ojukwu is an independent filmmaker and producer with a passion for storytelling. His journey into writing was inspired by his brother, Isaac Ojukwu, who took scriptwriting classes and encouraged Ike to explore his own creative potential.

Ike's love for writing spans across various genres, including horror, fiction, dark romantic stories, and even children's books. His diverse interests reflect his versatile storytelling abilities. One of his notable works is the zombie thriller "Shattered Dome: The Fight for Crescent City," which has captivated readers with its gripping narrative and intense action.

When Ike isn't immersed in writing or filmmaking, he enjoys traveling and experiencing new places. These adventures provide him with fresh perspectives and inspiration for his stories. His writing is infused with the belief that as long as you keep pushing, anything is possible—a message that resonates deeply with his readers.

"June to April: Bound by Obsession" is a product of Ike's personal experiences and the challenges he has faced in relationships. Through this heartfelt, dark love story, he aims to connect with readers who have undergone similar struggles, offering them a sense of understanding and hope.

Read more at www.k1films.com.

Milton Keynes UK
Ingram Content Group UK Ltd.
UKHW020022061124
450708UK00001B/294